NEW ANIMAL

New Animal

A novella

Eleanor Keisman

BROKEN TRIBE PRESS

ADVANCE PRAISE FOR *NEW ANIMAL*

"After reading *New Animal,* I can never again see the everyday sight of a person walking a dog without feeling uneasiness. What once seemed ordinary now appears heartbreakingly vulnerable—as climate disasters loom, even this simple pleasure might disappear at any time. Smelling the pheromones of animals throughout this sensuous novella, I was especially struck by its haunting portrayal of the bond between human and wolf: outwardly so different, yet alike in their lonely hunger for companionship. More precisely, they seek a companionship that is hierarchical rather than equal, for they aim to survive by all means, fair or foul. *New Animal* appears stoic on the surface, but underneath it pulses with raw desire and quiet desperation. The novella is cli-fi at its most profound: not merely describing environmental collapse, but exploring how it reshapes intimacies across species—an unforgettable work that lingers long after the final page."

—Chi Ta-wei, author of *The Membranes*

"Eleanor Keisman's *New Animal* is no polemic, it is not a call to action—it is a deeply emotional and stupendously powerful paean to the planet and all who depend on it. It is the sort of book that does more than simply make you think—although it does that—it makes you feel the sorts of things that we read great literature to feel: love, hate, empathy, and finally understanding.

While *New Animal* is the author's debut, it is the work of a remarkably mature writer in absolute mastery of her skills, of her vision, of the story she wants to tell. And though it is set against the backdrop of unthinkable world catastrophe, this story is underpinned by a constant note of hope, no matter how subtle it may be at times."

—Ted Flanagan, author of *Every Hidden Thing*

CONTENTS

"There is a patience of the wild – dogged, tireless, persistent as life itself."

—Jack London, *The Call of the Wild*

POPE

The snow had started to melt by early February.

The rapid approach of spring meant it had dripped from the boughs, refrozen to icicles over the cold night, and fallen into puddles when the morning air warmed. Most of the crows had left before the snow had fallen, and only a few stragglers remained. The chickadees were silent, and little tufts of green grass peeked out from leftover mounds of white, like an adolescent earth. The winter had begun so late that it wasn't clear if the grass had been there before it snowed and remained preserved in the frost, or had started to grow prematurely, in anticipation. Despite the shortness of winter, the season of slow starvation had been long. As he lapped water out of a clear, ice-cold stream, Pope hoped the new warmth would bring easy prey.

Soggy earth left over from the previous season padded the ground under Pope's feet as he trotted. After Pope and his mother and brother, the last of the Druid Pack, had been driven out of Yellowstone by the Fire of 2081, Pope headed north along the Rocky Mountains.

The summer had roasted, and this winter had clung shorter in duration than any in Pope's memory. He'd tried playing with his brother, and he'd bitten his face after he lay down, tired from the game of chase and withering of distemper. But Pope fled as his mother's eyes closed, the last to die, only a few months ago, bleeding from her mouth into the yellow and brown wet autumn leaves. This was the first spring he'd been alone, and the deer grazing lazily by the riverbanks knew it.

Not yet having shed its undercoat, Pope's black fur was thick and heavy, streaked by grey on his chest and belly and a white mask on his muzzle. Framed by two yellow eyes, rippling lines showed through the fur on his brow and snout: lines of weariness from losing his family, lines of bloodthirsty cunning, and lines of worry. Since the Great Fire, which took out the last northern territories of Yellowstone, Pope had searched for woods that felt like home.

But the Fire had shifted something in the climate, and that shift had followed him, changing the woods, the ebb and flow of the warmth and cold, the wet and the dry. The wolf calls dwindled, and an unnerving silence took their place. In the valleys, the streams had grown wider and drier as the numerous deer destroyed the banks. There were more beavers now, and their dams changed the flow of fresh water, limiting clean places for wolves to drink. The crows didn't call to him as they once did, their cooperative caws signaling food nearby. The deer were numerous now, and so were the elk, and because he had no pack to hunt them with, they were unafraid. He hadn't seen or heard another wolf since his mother died, and hunger and loneliness had come in her absence.

A note for the reader:

Wolves use particular sorts of growls to indicate friendship, respect, and reverence. A certain swish of the tail can indicate frustration or excitement, and a tucked tail can indicate fear and submission. The thumping of paw pads on the earth can be a sign of playfulness, and the lack of any sound is, of course, what prey animals hear, always too late, in the moments before they're slaughtered by a wolf pack. Within all these sounds, there could be clusters, habitual arrangements, that could be considered a name. A physical expression of a unique personality buried deep and often hardly noticeable to the bearer.

With that in mind, as long as Pope had been alive and existed in his own, personal state of awareness, the thump of his paw pads, the swish of his tail, and the sound of his own panting echoing inside his head, he heard:

P – Ahhh – Ppp – Uhh.

P – Ohh – P – Ehh.

P – Oh – P.

Pope.

Alone in the confusion of an early spring, Pope trod on, keeping the morning sun on his right side and felt the warmth of it cross his body over the course of the day. At the base of a larch, a sudden movement caught his eye. He froze and felt his mouth tighten, the skin on his back bunched together, and the muscles in his haunches gripped. He leapt into a silent sprint and in the space of two of his own heartbeats, he was upon it. Pope's fangs pierced the squirrel, and he tore at the flesh until it was gone, the delicious metallic smell of blood filling his nose. It was just a taste and made him even hungrier. Pope walked on until it was night, found some boulders hidden by brush, and bedded down. Craving more of the gritty blood coating his teeth, he did not sleep well.

He awoke to the sound of a crow's caw soaring across the air above, and for a moment, he wondered if his world had been set back to rights. Pope found a tree-lined creek with the bank intact, just like there used to be. Lapping the cool running water, he heard another sound awaken. He stopped drinking, face attentive, ears pricked. It was an intermittent whining, a somewhat recognizable song that went up and down and stopped and started again. Pope stood up straight. There was something of a howl in it, but it was dull, as though coming from something unwell and far away.

Every creature he'd encountered had some sound like this, some constellation of noises, but now, he heard something else, something dampened and less familiar. It was a murmur, gravelly and soft at the same time. The ground vibrated with the approaching movement of other life. His eyes darted to the brush just up the creek.

It stood there, staring at him, making the whining sound Pope had just heard, the one that came before the murmur. A bright pink tongue hung out to one side, and its breath was labored and smelled sweetly of fish. Pope's mouth began to water as he stared into its blue, vacant eyes. The snout was rounded and blunt, and its grey and black fur was fluffy, like a young rabbit. The coat was luscious, and it was well fed, perhaps even overfed, but there wasn't a trace of blood on its face. Pope saw the teeth: they were shorter than his, clean and dull.

The husky looked and sounded like Pope, perhaps when he was a small pup and before his mother had quieted him. But it was not at all a wolf. It was an unnatural copy, a thing Pope had never seen before.

The husky groaned again, and Pope understood what he'd heard in the sound. It was something wild that had long been cut and stifled.

Pope caught the smell of weeds burning, the brush rustled again, and a human stepped into the clearing. This was the first time he'd made eye contact with one, and he immediately dug in his feet and pulled back the corners of his mouth. The hair on his neck bristled. The human's shimmering eyes locked with Pope's as he dropped his cigarette in the creek, and the murmuring sound leaked from his mouth. He tugged the dog by the rope around its neck and began to back away slowly. The husky bucked and panted and made choking sounds. Pope stayed locked in position, his nostrils flaring as he inhaled the fear filling the space around him.

Pope watched the strange pair disappear behind the brush until he was completely alone by the creek. He stood frozen to the spot, uncertain of what he had just seen, until his body released at the familiar sound of a second crow caw. His jaw creaked open in a yawn, and he began patrolling the edge of the creek, checking into the woods beyond as he did.

The dog had looked like a distortion of the natural order of things, a bizarre deformity from some kind of sickness. But it was not like what he'd seen in his brother, the starvation and thirst that aged and crippled his body, no matter how much he ate or drank. His legs had grown thin and creaky, and when Pope slapped the ground, splayed his legs, and bowed, he'd only panted and drooled in response. Pope had taken special care to share more food with his mother, even though his brother yowled with hunger from the last place he'd ever lie. But his mother lasted a few days longer, and when he finally ran off, he wasn't sure if it was to avoid seeing her take her final breath, or to escape the rage he imagined rising off his brother's lifeless body.

Pope came to a tree that had fallen across the creek. He crossed to the other side and continued on, walking until the sun was directly overhead, hot sunlight slicing through the forest ceiling. A hum of cars began in the air. Pope didn't register this immediately, but it made it harder to spot softer sounds, like his own footsteps, which were heavy and sluggish. Pope fatigued as the air grew warmer, and he stopped to drink when there was water. He ate chipmunks and squirrels when he found them and followed the smell of blood when he caught it, though it often led to animals that had been dead far too long. Pope felt his skin stretching tight across his ribcage when he took a deep breath. The sound of cars grew steadily, and the flavor of burning exhaust filled the air. He was unsettled to realize it was a sound he'd heard once before, a sound which he would have once done anything to evade.

The forest began to thin, and the terrain grew steep. Just as Pope wondered if he should turn back, he heard familiar sounds like the ones by the creek. Wolf pup-like yelps and howls, again with the soul taken out of them, mixed with low grunts and murmurs, human sounds.

Pope came to the crest of a hill. He was panting, and it was the warmest he'd ever felt at this time of year. And as his pink tongue shook from quick, shallow gasps, he wondered if it was breathlessness or shock that made his heartbeat vibrate through his entire body.

From the tree line, the valley sloped down, a black road cutting through the center, the roar of cars filling the space like an echo chamber. Next to the road, and closer to Pope, was a dog park, the grass spotted with dead and yellowing patches of grass. Humans milled inside, and around them, rapid, swirling clusters of dogs. But just as Pope had been bewildered by the husky in the forest, not understanding that it was a domesticated dog, his eyes were unable to make sense of the scene he saw before him. Flashes of greys, yellows, browns, whites, and blacks of varying sizes ricocheted from one end of the enclosure to the other, occasionally colliding with one another, and shooting back and forth once again. It was from these animals that Pope heard the familiar, yet broken, yelps and howls. Sounds which, because they were *almost* right, were entirely wrong; chaotic calls, with anything that was once wild in them removed. The dogs played like he and his brother had, but they were frantic and clumsy. They looked like animals infected with a sickness that struck down not a single life, but an entire line. It frightened Pope because, in watching them, the bizarre creature in the woods took on a new form: The husky was him, copied to extinction.

He stumbled and snapped a twig, froze, and looked intently toward the valley. Pope was certain he'd been heard, but the humans and animals made no reaction. One of the humans whistled. The dogs ran to form a circle, and Pope's mouth watered at the sight of the crude formation: The humans had food. The dogs had food. Pope's body urged him to retreat and to run back to the woods. But his head pounded from hunger, and stronger than the din of cars, and more provocative than the calls from the dogs, an enticing smell filled the air. The smell of cooked, charred meat seemed to seek out Pope's nose, beckoning him nearer.

Pope stalked the edge of the tree line, staying out of sight. It was odd to be this close to creatures that weren't aware of his presence. Even a rabbit would smell something in the air and grow tense. He broke from the trees and trotted silently down to the enclosure, slowing to a crawl as one of the dogs turned to look at him. This one looked more like him, more wolfish. But it was smaller in the body, narrower in the head, and had browner fur. There was a vacant look in its eyes, which were dark brown and slightly unevenly sized. It had no lines of fury, fear, or cunning. For just a moment, it occurred to Pope that it wasn't vacancy he saw in its eyes, but softness. It was not a look Pope had seen before, and it was not one he recognized as fit to survive. But this creature had found a reliable way to get food, and Pope had not. It stood there staring at him, one ear flopped to the side, with its pink tongue hanging out, bobbing as it panted. It was not a wolf. But it was a wolf. It *was*, at some point.

Pope quickly took in the rest of the scene: He saw dogs that looked dwarfed with blocky patches of color, that had tiny heads and tinier bodies, and that looked more like dandelion tufts than animals – beagles and toy poodles. And he was still more horrified to see others that seemed to have no noses, with eyes peering out from their necks – French bulldogs. They looked at him and wheezed, their tongues sloppily flapping against a snoutless stump.

He watched as a large poodle ran with a round object, bringing it back to a human. The poodle dropped the ball, and the human picked it up and threw it away. The dog seemed excited to run after it, retrieving it and bringing it back again. To Pope's confusion, this continued repeatedly. A border collie sat nearby, watching. Pope assumed the black and white animal was just as confused until it got up, ran to another corner of the enclosure, found a stick, and brought it to the same human, who swatted the border collie away.

The sound of a whimper drew Pope's attention back to the gentle-eyed creature in front of him. The Doberman-mutt had pulled its tongue inside its mouth, and the space between the unevenly sized brown eyes was wrinkled and raised in a look Pope recognized as one of expectation. It nodded its elongated head, released a breathy, somewhat high-pitched, metallic-smelling bark, and slapped the ground. Pope felt the vibration.

Pp-hap-ppp.

Pope flapped his ears forward and back. He picked up one paw to slap the ground in reply, but paused in mid-air, and then placed it down without force. Instead of a bark, he only managed a frustrating whimper. The mutt continued to watch Pope curiously, but when one of the humans whistled, it bolted off and away from Pope. He followed its path and caught the eyes of one of the humans. Instead of quivering, as the man in the woods had, he saw, behind the look of surprise, a calm mastery in the face. It was the same look his mother had given his brother when he stepped out of line. It was in the unspoken message shared between the pack just before they attacked their prey, and it was confirmed for Pope in that moment: These creatures *had* once been wolves, until the humans had interfered with them. He had seen the remains of wolves torn to shreds by moose antlers, ravaged by bears, and once hit by a car, when the pack had ventured too far to the edge of the woods. But he had never seen this. He lowered his head, stumbled, and panted, his mouth parched from thirst, and the air's smoky scent.

A piece of meat came sailing through the air, and Pope pounced on it, swallowing it nearly whole. Another, much larger piece, landed near him. Unlike the prey Pope was used to feasting on, the cooked meat was free of fur, skin, and sinew, and instead of feeling slippery and tough, it crumbled grittily in his mouth.

Pope startled from a piercing bang. A man ran from the far side of the field toward the enclosure. He was shouting, and he had a pistol in his hands. The humans and their dogs swirled and shifted farther away from Pope. The running man came closer to Pope and just as he fired the pistol another time, a second man pounced, and both tumbled to the ground. Pope turned to bolt toward the woods, but his front legs found nothing but air as his neck and head were jerked back by a cord. It tightened, and Pope's vision closed in.

A DESPERATE CALL AND RESPONSE

Pope woke up surrounded by metal bars on a moving platform.

He couldn't read signs, but if he could, he'd have seen the words BEAVER SPRING KENNELS as the pickup truck pulled into the facility. His head bobbed up and down, and he felt the contents of his stomach shift. He'd never been in a car before, but he'd seen them, moving faster than any animal could gallop. Picking up one front paw and placing it back down again, he felt too unsteady to get up. The smell in the air stung his nostrils; it was the smell of another animal's sickness and waste, and it was not fresh.

The moving platform came to a stop, and Pope heard murmurs once again, the sound he now recognized as humans. Metal creaked and banged as his cage door opened. Pope's upper lip curled, revealing his sharp and forbidding fangs as he met the cold eyes of a man holding a catchpole.

"This one's a devil. You got the gun ready?"

"Yup, 50mg all set."

"Come here with the other stick, he's gonna bite my balls off if I'm not careful."

Pope felt a cable slip over his head and tighten around his neck, and then another just the same. He tried to dig his claws into the ground underneath him, but there was only slippery metal. Confused as to why he couldn't do anything to oppose, Pope was led out of the cage by two men, each holding catchpoles.

He couldn't lunge and overtake them, or back away, or run. He roared and jerked his head from side to side, but couldn't move as his muscles demanded. The cord sliced into his neck, and the more he strained, the tighter the men held. They pushed and tugged him into another small space, enclosed by metal bars on a concrete slab. It was one of a row of cages, enclosed by concrete walls on all sides except for wire cage doors. The men slipped the catchpole cables off Pope's neck, slammed his cage door shut, and pelted him with hard pieces of something that smelled like sweet, regurgitated meat. The kibble littered the floor, some falling into a metal bowl of water covered with a thin layer of scum.

Pope remained standing for a long time, periodically adjusting his paw pads against the hard concrete. He felt his body brace against something else: A plaintive noise, an infantile howling that made his fur bristle and his spine lock. The view from his cage looked only on a concrete pathway and a grassy field, so he couldn't see where the sound was coming from, but it filled the air. It was a wolfish sound, but far removed from the pack chatter he knew. Higher pitched and more panicked than the wolf yelps, groans, and growls that he'd known, these sounds had a sound of desperation in them. They made something inside him twitch uncomfortably, as though a part of him were sprinting, or would be if he could. The twitch grew bigger than him, making him shiver under its pressure. He groaned sharply, once, twice, and then the groan became a nervous howl, and the sound of it carried through the kennel, reaching ears that regarded it only with curious wonder.

Over the next few days, Pope slept, ate, and was largely left alone. It was March, and the rains came earlier than the previous year. Pope's cage was kept dry, unexposed to the elements. A few times, when Pope woke in the night, during a few quiet hours when the rest of the kennel was asleep, he watched as snow flurries drifted in aimlessly and out of place, a final reprieve of a dying winter. He remembered the joy on his brother's face during their first winter, how they'd played and rolled in the fresh powder. They had seen only one more white season together.

Compared to the months of solitude he'd spent in the forests, the loneliness Pope felt in the kennel was instant and penetrating. All around him were sounds of animals which, to him, sounded wolfish, but with the "wild" somehow removed. Occasionally, he would yelp and groan in response, but he came to notice different accents in the sounds, accents he couldn't match or fully understand. It overwhelmed him and intensified his need to chatter, to run, to meet the eyes of another creature, to hope to be understood.

On the fifth day in the kennel, Pope heard a commotion. He stood upright, tail straight and ears alert. He sniffed and tasted the air, and despite the yelling of the humans, he smelled something familiar. Something pungent, metallic, the musk of his puppyhood. Certain that another wolf was nearby, he began to pace, and the pacing became a frenzy. Had he been outside and free, it would have been a gallop of anticipation and hopeful exhilaration. But as it was, trapped in a cage, he whirled and bounced in the small enclosure, whipping himself until he froze in position, alert to what he heard: A wolf howl. Pope groaned, and the groan grew louder until it became a desperate, raspy howl. An answer came, and Pope was swept once again into a frenzy. A man rushed near his cage.

"Alright, quiet now!" He fumbled with some keys and moved to unlock Pope's cage.

Pope ripped through the cage door, knocked the man to the ground, and ran along the row of cages. He let out a call, and the call was returned. He sprinted with joy and uncertainty as he passed the other kennel cages. They were filled with creatures like the ones he'd seen in the dog park, of strange sizes and mixes of colors. Some screeched and some bellowed, but above it all, he heard the howl. It had an accent to it, a strange tenor, and was different from the wolf calls he'd known. But he understood and was understood in return. The pair synchronized together, a call and response of fear, loneliness, confusion, and captivity. Most of all, the calls were filled with a longing for something the other dogs knew nothing about.

He bolted from one row of kennels to another, quick on his feet despite hunger and days of eating a barely tolerable, waxy kibble. He heard men shouting and knew they were close. He knew that unless he could find his way far away from this place, his escape would be short-lived. He smelled tree sap in the surroundings, but everywhere he looked were wire fences, standing higher than he could jump. Dog chatter and whining came from all sides, the sounds spreading wider than he could run.

As if his snout had been grabbed by an unknown energy, Pope's head snapped to the right. He could see a man, towering in height, his chest rising and falling with each breath, adjusting his grip around the tranquilizer gun as he locked his gaze. Pope heard another call, this time from mere steps away, and his head was tugged in its direction, one survival instinct fighting another. Without a conscious choice, Pope had taken his eyes off the man with the gun and looked now into a cage, into a pair of light-yellow eyes.

This creature was smaller than he'd expected. The fur was a brown-grey mix, and the snout was thinner. It stood shorter than Pope. Its tongue lolled out, and it yelped with the same accent that had been in the howls. Though Pope was thin from hunger, and he stood taller, thicker, and stronger than the wolfdog, he felt a surge of familial warmth come from within. He wanted to move closer, sniff the cage, lick the air. He wanted the animal to break out and for them to run together toward the trees, playing and jumping on each other, killing prey as hunger came. He wanted to learn the accent of the wolfdog, and to teach his own accent in return. Pope's legs twitched as though living out these fantasies in a waking dream. But he didn't move from the spot because he knew he was surrounded. He sorrowfully broke his gaze from the wolfdog and turned back to the reality of his captivity.

"That's a good boy."

"You got the tranq ready?"

"Block off the back."

Pope watched as the tall man with the gun approached, but it wasn't until another man's boot scuffed the concrete in Pope's rear that he began to snarl, ears pulled back, fur bristling. The smell of fear filled the air once again, but this time, it belonged to Pope. The wolfdog began groaning and huffing.

"Shut that dog up!"

"Shoot him already!"

Pope felt the sting in his hind quarters, a loop going around his neck, and his body hitting the earth all at once. His eyes closed as men's voices encircled him, and though he was trapped, he felt a part of himself running free, leaping with joy. He didn't know this animal, but he knew it was more of a wolf than any other creature he'd recently encountered, and he rested a little more easily, having a flicker of hope restored.

That night, as he slept on the cold floor of the kennel, Pope had a dream that he wouldn't remember. He dreamt of being very small and curled up inside a soft bed, like a snow cave warmed from the cuddling bodies of he and his brother when they were pups. But it was drier than a snow cave and made of the wool of another animal. The bed sat on a wooden floor, warm from the fire behind him. The sound of crackles tingled inside his head like one of nature's lullabies. Shadows flickered on the walls, sometimes as high as the ceiling, where wood beams held up the roof of the triangle-shaped cabin. The shadows made shapes he felt he recognized, but from what origin, he could not place. An orange blaze from the sunrise outside gently sliced the shadows from the fire, and they grew short and dim as the morning took over the dawn. His fur was dry, and his mouth was wet, as though he'd just eaten. The sweet musk of hairless flesh mixed with the smell of smoke piqued his attention as two black boots strode past him, vibrating the floor with each step.

"Come on, Shirl," said a man's voice.

Pope's ears pricked to the sound of claws clattering. Streaks of white and brown shot past him, and his nose filled with something familiar, something close to him, but also something very far away. It was a smell that – even asleep, he knew this – he had not been near for a long time. It both delighted and preoccupied him, as when the brain tries to fill in the missing pieces of a puzzle it doesn't know how to solve but doesn't understand unsolved. There was a pink tongue, the sound of happy panting, and a deep groan. Pope heard the crunch of incisors and smelled something woody and sweet mingled with the pungent tang of saliva. A door somewhere creaked open, and he squinted at the sudden gust of cold air that rushed past the silhouette of a human and a wolf.

"Gonna be a big snow again later today, let's see if we can't find any critters hole up in the wood pile."

Even though the pair were visible only in outline, and no features were apparent, the color of the human's red shirt was as clear as bloody mud, and as promising a sight as a warm meal. The man pulled a Stetson from a rack on the wall. He fixed it on his head, turned to the wolf, and patted his chest. The wolf laughed and reared, throwing its paws against the wood-planked floor.

"You're a damn fool sometimes, Shirley girl."

He patted his chest again, and once again the wolf reared up, high enough for her paws to rest on the man's shoulders. He braced himself against her weight.

"Easy, easy there."

Tilting her head up and groaning, her snout reached higher even than the tip of his Stetson. The man grunted in reply, an odd sound with a strange accent. It was an attempt to copy an alien language in sound only, with no concept of what meaning the sounds built. Nevertheless, the wolf called Shirley recognized the attempt as well-meaning, and she grunted and softly nibbled his face in response.

Pope wanted to bite the wolf's legs and jump on top of her, to be picked up by this human, struggle, and howl until he was put down again, only to nip at his feet, hoping to be lifted up once more. He wanted to stand up and follow them, to follow the colors of brown and dark red, to remain with the reassuring smells of furry and furless musk. He wanted to, and he tried to, but he couldn't. He willed himself to move a single paw, but no part of him would move, and the harder he tried, the fuzzier everything became, and the colder he felt, until all he felt was the kennel concrete below him. Pope's eyes opened to a low sun, just rising, as a man silhouetted in light approached his cage door.

Unlike the others who had come near to feed and water him, and of course, the three men who muscled him into the cage, this man did not have a clearly outlined head. Humans Pope had seen were upright, fleshy, four-limbed things, with small, snoutless heads. Sometimes they wore hats, and other times they didn't. But the proportions of this man were different, and Pope could see that, even in outline alone. As the man approached, he became more clearly visible: He was shorter than the others, which rooted him lower to the ground. His hands were large, oversized as if on a young pup. But this man was not particularly young, and he seemed to grow into his hands as he moved, becoming perfect ends to his thick arms. He looked unbound, like a wilding tree, escaping its confinement and hanging heavy with bulbous fruits under a looming canopy. In silhouette, his head was obscured by shoulder-length, bushy hair, and the wild man's round face was nearly lost in a great feral mane.

Pope sniffed the air and pawed at his eyes, and the memory of the dream evaporated, like a burnt summer puddle. He felt groggy, confused, and slow to wake. It had been days since he'd had the taste of blood in his mouth, and the kibble he'd been given did not contain the nourishment he was used to.

"Careful, Bill. We just got that one in. Went on a rampage yesterday."

The wild man knelt next to Pope's cage and put his fingers against the bars.

"Jesus, Bill, care—"

"Easy there, just relax, ok?"

A low rumble came from Pope, and he felt the skin on his back bristle. His fur rippled, and his upper lip tightened over his fangs. Never dropping eye contact with the wild man, he edged himself to the back corner of his cage, belly hugging the ground. *Easy there.* Pope knew the sounds in that call, the softness of it residing somewhere in the back of his memory, though he didn't understand the meaning. He growled, his nostrils flaring as the uncannily familiar smell of the wild man filled the cage.

POPE AND THE WILD MAN

"You can't leave him in there alone."

The wild man's voice was the one thing Pope could single out from the cacophony of what sounded like dying creatures around him. Animals with traces of wild in them from generations before, snuffed and stifled to the point of a kind of existential starvation. Sounds he'd heard in the dog park, only filled with more desperation and chaos. The pitchy howls, the moaning, and the incessant staccato barking – something between inexperienced wolf pups complaining for food, and grown wolves mourning and consoling one another after a pack member's death.

It had been two days of noise for Pope, two days since he'd seen an animal that was anything close to a wolf. It was a symphony of sadness that made his ears ache and his belly feel hollow in a way no amount of food could fill. He no longer howled, and no longer heard any howl. With his eyes closed, body tucked in a protective coil, all sounds blended together. The only disruption came from the feel of a cable dragging over his muzzle.

"Hey, that dog's wild.

"You bet he's wild. That's a wolf, and like I said – you can't leave him in there alone."

"Ain't no wolves no more, Bill."

The cable tightened, the cage door opened wider, and Pope begrudgingly hoisted himself to his feet. His upper lip quivered, as if to bare his teeth, and his throat clenched, as if for a growl. But he didn't complete either of those actions: There was that voice again, something he felt he knew, but couldn't recall how. There was something in it that reminded him of his mother, that made him think of his home in Yellowstone, before the Fire.

The truth was, he couldn't recall very much of his young life in Yellowstone, and what he could came to him only in dreams. And then it was a collage of strange, wishful images: fires that didn't destroy, men that didn't pursue and crowd in on wolf territory, and walls that didn't cage. He dreamt sometimes of his mother, how her face would appear in the damp darkness of the den she'd made for Pope and his brother, when they were very small. But in the dense reality of waking life, all he could ever bring up of Yellowstone was the heat and the dryness. And then the Fire, which erupted out of a forest, devoured a lake and then everything else in its path, and sent Pope and his pack, and every other wolf pack and non-human and human creature, out of Yellowstone forever.

Pope was led out of his cage and past a row of more cages. He kept his head down and his ears pulled back and tried to ignore the riot of sounds. The concrete felt unforgiving, and his claws clicked against it as he placed each paw down. But at least it was cool and not yet warmed by the sun. The nights had the chill of a late winter, and mornings and evenings held the spring air comfortably. But during the days, the temperature of the kennel rose with the unnaturalness of a summer arriving prematurely. Pope was always elated for the arrival of winter, and despaired each year it left, sooner than the last. Feeling the heat build throughout the days over the past days, Pope felt it was the end of winter, as he knew it, forever.

Pope stepped onto the grass and was momentarily surprised and delighted by the familiar softness under his weight, which hadn't increased much since he'd been in the kennel. He lifted his head and squinted in the sunlight. The wild man had led him away from the row of cages and into a small field, the far corner of which was caged off. He stopped walking and seemed to take notice of the grass himself, rocking back and forth on his feet. Pope smelled a change in him, an ease, which in turn eased Pope. He heard the wild man take a deep breath, and his body expanded and contracted, taking up more space than it did a few moments prior, growing in the sun. Pope raised his head up higher, unexpectedly meeting the man's gaze. It was as masterful and terrifying as a bear, and as open as the most devoted pack member. The wild man led Pope, who carried himself with a little more ease, across the grass.

The fenced area was shaded by a large tree and several haystacks piled on top of one another. What was sitting next to the haystacks, Pope smelled before he saw: a wolfdog, the same one he'd encountered two days before. If Pope could have answered the question, *How do you know it's a wolfdog, and not a full wolf?*, he might have said that it had to do with the size of his body, the fullness of his fur, the shape of his snout, his eye and fur color. He'd say that he remembered the wolfdog's strangely pitched and accented howls and grunts. He might have also said that it simply smelled different, and though it was the first wolfdog he'd ever seen, he just knew that it was something *other.*

The wild man watched as Pope sniffed and tasted the air, as his skin rippled across his back, over his bony shoulder blades. He watched as the wolfdog stood up inside the enclosure, ears directed forward, licking Pope's scent in the air, and slightly smiling the way dogs often do. Then the wild man started howling. He began softly with a low note, and the note grew wider and louder and higher. He did it repeatedly until the wolfdog joined in.

Though it felt forced and awkward, and though the wolf-howls coming from two non-wolves were accented and foreign, Pope was powerless against the urge to join in. A low sound emerged from deep within him, and finding a higher pitch, he called back. It was a deep, sonorous howl that seemed to stop time in the space where they stood. And perhaps it was a natural reverence for a true wild howl, but as Pope's call soared, the man's grew softer and so did the wolfdog's, allowing Pope to lead the three of them in a heartfelt song.

BILL AND THE WOLF

Beaver Spring was a small Canadian town, nestled in a valley near the Alaskan border, and at one time, in the surrounding forests, wolf calls were a common sound. A very long time ago, they were a threatening sound, a call for men to get their guns, to shoot to kill, to wipe out entire family lines, an entire pack's culture gone in a flash. Wolves went truly wild for a time after that. There were no elders to teach the young how and where to hunt. There was no information to pass down, and wolves ventured too far into the world of men, and the population thinned to near extinction.

But the wolf calls eventually returned, and wolves and humans managed to exist without interfering with one another. No man crossed the borders determined by Fish and Wildlife, and wolves stayed in wolf territory. But every once in a while, a pack would cross the boundaries during a hunt. Or a lone wolf, seeking a pack of his own, would wander into human territory and, because it was easy prey, kill a livestock animal.

Were the boundaries too small? Had human beings underestimated the need for wolves to seek out new territory, to see a hunt through to its natural end? And as for the livestock, had farmers created a new form of slavery in those animals, a slave so valuable that the punishment for its destruction is death? The peaceful existence between men and wolves didn't last long. Recognizing the power of the wolf, and perhaps fearing its freedom in a world where animals were subjugated, men got a yearning to dominate the natural order once more.

"Hey, that dog's wild.

"You bet he's wild. That's a wolf, and like I said – you can't leave him in there alone."

"Ain't no wolves no more, Bill."

Bill tightened the cable around the wolf's neck and led him out of the cage. It felt unnatural for him to handle a wolf in this way, but that wasn't the only thing about the Beaver Spring Kennel that felt unnatural. On the surface, they advertised as a boarding kennel and adoption shelter, a place to house pets when owners were out of town, and for prospective dog owners to browse dogs that needed a home. But the kennel advertised to the wealthy, and because of that, it was more of a breeding facility than anything else.

The deadly intensity of the seasons had made it harder for people to go outside with any confidence. They didn't know when they'd get caught in a torrential storm or a sudden heat wave that melted the rubber on their shoes. Dogs became less a hiking and hunting companion and more a personal trophy. Mutts, despite their typically lovable temperaments, were no longer popular, and although the kennel said they were a "no-kill" shelter, they didn't keep their word when it came to mixed breeds that had been at the shelter far too long. More and more often, the mutts also died from heat. People wanted designer dog breeds, and the more exotic the breed, the greater the value.

Since the changed ecosystem had led to a nearly demolished wolf population – some thought they were altogether extinct – wolfdogs were an increasingly desirable breed.

It was late morning, but the valley still held some cool air from the night. Bill's curly hair puffed out from under his ball cap and hung down to just above his shoulders. They'd been strict about that at Yellowstone, making guides keep their appearance tidy. It seemed unnecessary to him; the animals didn't care if he had long hair. He was a Neo-Abolitionist, and most of them had long hair. It was their poetic way of showing solidarity with the animals, a symbol of the wild still alive within modern men. But none of that mattered since the Great Fire of 2081 had sent him north, looking for work, any place he could find it.

Bill led the wolf toward the mating enclosure, and his stomach turned just at the sight of it.

He felt both an intense disgust for what the kennel did and a guilty curiosity. It was true that man had bastardized the grand nature of the domesticated dog. Mankind had reached its hand in and rewired the genome of a once glorious animal, producing a variety of abnormal features and genetic physical problems that got worse with each litter of a breed. These dogs were damned to a life of suffering, caged inside a body that heard the call of the wild, but could not answer.

But wolves were going extinct, and the natural balance was suffering in their absence. Prey animals like deer, moose, and elk had become numerous, and they ate away at the landscape, stripping the grass and vegetation. One of the Neo-Abolitionists' goals was to rewild wolves, but the skewing of the seasons, the severity of the summers, and the shortening of the winters made it a Sisyphean feat. The wolves were dying, and there might never be enough to set things right again. But there could be enough wolfdogs, the last remaining link in the wolf lineage. If enough of their primal instinct remained, they might be able to take their ancestors' place in the wild.

Bill and the wolf stopped on the grass. He rocked himself back and forth on his feet and noticed out of the corner of his eye that the wolf mimicked him, as if reacquainting himself with the ground once more. Bill felt the sun warm his face. It had just peeked over the side of the valley and hung lower in the sky than it should for the kind of heat that had become normal for March. His nostrils twitched, and he realized he was smelling wolf breath. He looked down and saw the wolf, cruelly restrained in the catchpole he was forced to use, sniffing the air, the wild nostrils palpitating.

He looked over at the wolfdog who had started doing the same thing. Both male animals licked the air, and the wolfdog smiled. Bill could see a recognition between the two of them, but they were still, in their very core, of a different nature. A wolf was subject to no one except another wolf, and one false move, one misinterpreted sound, one strange smell, would spark him to react. The wolf was too valuable to Bill to risk it being put down, and the wolfdog was too valuable to the kennel not to put a wolf down the moment it behaved violently – this kind of value, of course, being completely meaningless to domesticated and wild animals alike.

But wolf behavior wasn't nearly as unpredictable as a wolfdog's. A wolf in its natural environment, within a pack structure, was a predictable animal. It was easy to know where and what it would hunt, which wolf would track, and which would distract, and which would make the final kill. A wolf pack left alone to live in peace was anything but a threat to a farmer's livestock. They wouldn't hunt what wasn't in their territory. A man could learn how to behave around a wolf, and what behaviors and sounds could be threatening.

A man *could* learn, but there were few left who would.

A wolfdog was an entirely different creature, manufactured by humans and therefore had no place in the natural order. Part dog, it could behave as a companion to man, submissive and eagerly obedient. But one never knew when the amber-eyed wolf at the core of its being would awaken.

Uncertain as Bill was that the wolf would accept the wolfdog as a member of the same family, he had to try to acquaint them, and the mating enclosure was the best place in the kennel for a private introduction. Though wolves make many sounds, there was one sound Bill knew well: the howl. To some, it sends a chill down the spine, and to others, like Bill, it signaled a reverence for something free and untamed, and a sadness for something slowly going extinct. Feeling like a translator, Bill began to howl in the best way he knew how.

At first, his howl rested in his natural speaking place, deep and low, but he pushed it up to a higher note and sent it sailing through the air. The wolfdog let out a few yelps and then joined in with his own call. And next to him, Bill saw the wolf's bony ribcage lurch, as though the howl were not a conscious choice, but an involuntary emission, a call to something greater than the three of them. It was eloquent and solemn, and in the presence of such mastery, Bill and the wolfdog quieted, only slightly, as the wolf led them in a monotone, yet mellifluous chant of the wild.

BECAUSE THEY WERE FAMILY

Bill grew up down the street from a girl called Shirley.

Shirley's family lived in a house in Queens, something that hadn't been common for a long time. Their family had owned it for generations, and they managed it, even though the house was crumbling in places, the roof blistered and frayed from roasting in the hot Northeastern summers. Bill's family lived nearby on the 19th floor of a 20-story building. There was no green space, not of the sort Bill had heard his grandparents speak.

They told him of neighborhood parks, filled with real grass, where people had something called *picnics,* where they ate lunch outside when the weather was warm, because the ground wasn't yet too hot to sit on, nor was noon in July too hot to go outside – although it soon would be. They told him about hiking in the mountains, the Catskills they were called, before they were leveled, piece by piece, to make room for settlements of city dwellers trying to escape the heat. Bill watched them get misty-eyed as they told stories of eating sandwiches outside, taking shelter under trees in the rain, the sound of leaves squishing underfoot and the very specific sweet smell of wet dirt. Bill listened and tried to imagine a world he'd never seen before.

Bill's childhood summers were spent inside, each one stretching out longer than the last one, to the point that the forbidding heat of the season overlapped with the fall school semester. By the time he was a teenager, September was largely spent in his room, having lessons taught from a computer screen. The double-layered windows were always sealed, and centralized air was pumped into the entire building between the hours of 10 am and 6 pm. The doors to the building were automatically locked just after 10 am and unlocked again a few minutes after 6 pm. Between 6:30 and 7:30 pm, a small domed playground with a jungle gym, swings, and a sandbox opened down the street, halfway between Bill's apartment building and Shirley's house. When Bill was young, like most children in the neighborhood, he was allowed to go and play, and so was Shirley, and that's how they met.

Each child entered the playground one at a time, and over each tiny body, a disinfectant mist rained down. Most children had no allergic reactions to the spray, but some did, and they had to stop coming. Bill once saw a friend break out into hives from the spray, and he didn't see him at the playground again. *What do the other kids do, the ones stuck at home?* Bill wondered this often, as he pumped his legs on the swing, or flung sand at other children, the grains sticking to damp flesh and digging into knees as they tripped and fell on the spongy rubberized floor. He thought about his days inside with his family on weekends, or shut in the school building during weekdays. The hours blended together, and sometimes he wasn't even sure how *he* passed the time. There was coloring. There was reading. There was TV. There were the chores his parents made him do. Meals helped to break up the monotony.

But none of that could add up to nine hours locked inside on school days, and eight hours locked inside on Saturdays and Sundays. It had been this way as long as Bill could remember, but even at age ten, the artificiality of it was apparent to him. The weather was temperate enough only for a few months in fall, winter, and spring for the doors to unlock and for people to move freely. November through the end of February was a joyful time, even if it was spent in the towering concrete forest that had become all five boroughs of New York City.

One June, when Bill was eight, he spent the weekend in jail with his grandmother.

The two sat in the air-conditioned kitchen, at the table, drinking glasses of barley tea. Bill swung his legs back and forth, the trademark itchiness of a restless child from a day spent inside a classroom. She disliked intensely to see him so filled with energy that had no place to go, and she wanted to entertain him, so she told him all about the picnics her family had gone on when she was a girl and how his grandfather had proposed to her. "He picked me up in front of my house. Most of us lived in houses then, not like it is now. Apartment buildings were mostly in Manhattan, not this far out in Queens. I remember my neighbor's uncle lived in an apartment building in Manhattan. He lived above a dentist and got special rates on dental cleanings. Back then, things like that were more expensive."

"I hate the dentist."

"You'd hate it more if you couldn't afford one! Anyway, I remember it was a hot summer day. Not hot like it is now, but still, it could get uncomfortable. I remember once, walking barefoot in the house, my feet got so sweaty that I slipped and fell!"

"Grandma..." Bill squirmed with impatience.

"Sorry, honey, where was I? He knocked on my door – you could just knock then, and people in the house would hear. The walls weren't so thick. Anyway, he knocked on my door, and when I opened it, there he was with a picnic basket. He reminded me of my father. I was so excited to see him. Not about the picnic so much – he gave me such butterflies that I lost my appetite! But we sat on the grass – real grass, Billy! We sat on the grass, surrounded by other picnickers. We had cake with eggs in it, lemonade, and when I picked up my ham sandwich – which was neatly made and perfectly cut in half – there was a diamond ring poking out, gleaming in the sunlight."

"What's ham?"

"Oh, don't worry about that. It's just something we used to eat that we don't anymore."

"Can't we go on a *pinksnic* too? Just like that one?"

"*Picnic*, dear. Oh my, that would be complicated now. There are a lot more rules nowadays than when I was young."

But Bill's grandmother couldn't remember all the rules. She couldn't remember that people weren't allowed to eat outside in a city. It wasn't the eating; it was how wide a person was allowed to open their mouths. Children weren't allowed to scream on the playground, and if anyone started crying, they had to be taken home immediately. Respiratory viruses had mutated, and people weren't permitted to leave their homes if they were sick. No one had picnics anymore. But Bill didn't know any of this, or if he did, he needed someone to remind him, in the way that children need to be reminded of things constantly before they can commit them to permanent memory. Things like: Don't run in the street. Stop playing with your food. Stand up straight. Clean your room. Do your homework. Things that parents say but grandparents rarely do.

"Come on, grandma. Please?"

Bill knew his grandmother missed his grandfather. The man had died when Bill was only five, but he could remember the two of them together. They lived with Bill and his mother and father, and he always remembered them holding hands. Even at the dinner table. If Bill dropped his napkin or fork and crawled down to get it, he'd see them holding hands, his grandmother to the right and his grandfather to the left. He wondered if each had had opposing handedness, and this was how they were able to hold hands and eat at the same time. He asked his grandmother this once. She said that she didn't know if he'd been born left-handed, but he always ate that way. She smiled when she said this, a smile that seemed to carry her off to another place. Bill wished he could see where those smiles took her, but that might have also been because he was so antsy from being stuck inside.

At 6:15 pm the next day, which was a Friday, Bill left the house as soon as the doors were unlocked. The sun wouldn't set for a few more hours, and the warm air hit his face with the concentration of damp fabric. Even though the humidity made breathing difficult, he sprinted down his street, past two other tall apartment buildings. His grandmother was making protein oatcakes to bring to the playground, and he couldn't wait to tell Shirley. His grandmother always put in raisins, and Shirley had once told him that she loved raisins, although he'd never actually seen her eat one. He rounded the corner and continued down two more blocks where the buildings grew shorter, until he came to a street that had only houses, and finally to Shirley's house. Doors to houses were locked on a slightly different timer than apartment buildings, and Bill had to wait outside until Shirley could open the door. Bill stood on the stoop, still baking from the heat of the day, and the two made faces at each other through the double-paned window until Bill finally heard the *click* of the lock.

"You look like a clown," said Shirley, pulling the curly hair that poked out of the sides of Bill's ball cap.

"You've never seen a clown." Bill tried to tuck his hair behind his ears, but it popped right back out. His mother hadn't given him a haircut in what felt like a month, but it was probably closer to several months.

"What's a picnic taste like?"

"It's not *something* you eat; it's *how* you eat. It's when you eat food outside. My grandma said so." Bill was hopping back and forth from one foot to the other. "Hurry up, let's go! She's making oatcakes."

"Mommy, I'm going to the playground, ok?"

Shirley pulled a bucket hat over her short, straight black hair, slipped canvas shoes on her feet, and pulled on one of the government-issued UV jackets hanging by the door.

"Put on sunscreen!" Her mother called from somewhere in the back of the house.

"I'm wearing my jacket!" Shirley let the door slam behind her.

Bill's grandmother waved to them from a patch of artificial grass around the corner of the entrance to the playground. There weren't any other people there, but that's because people didn't sit outside on grass anymore. "This would make a good spot!"

She put down a blanket, and it floated awkwardly atop the plastic grass, which poked up like little toothpicks. It was purely aesthetic, not made for walking on. At his grandmother's insistence, Bill and Shirley sat down on the blanket. The plastic felt warm and pokey underneath them and they shifted their legs underneath their bodies, trying to get comfortable.

"I don't have any lemonade or sandwiches, but we'll have to make do. I don't think you've ever tried one of my oatcakes, Shirley! Billy tells me you like raisins."

"I'm not supposed to eat other people's food."

"Gimme it!" Bill snatched an oatcake out of his grandmother's hand.

"Manners, William!"

Bill angled his body away from Shirley, reached into his pocket, and pulled out a toy ring with a plastic garnet-colored stone. He tucked it into the oatcake, and it blended in perfectly with the raisins. He looked up to see his grandmother wink at him. "Give Shirley her oatcake now, honey." She stroked Bill's cheek.

Shirley hesitated as she reached to take the oatcake. Just before it touched her fingers, someone shouted.

"Hey!"

Shirley took the oatcake.

"Hey, you can't do that! Stop! Drop that!" A policeman in a standard-issue gas mask came over and grabbed Shirley's arm, knocking the oatcake to the ground. Shirley looked up, and her lip quivered.

"My mom said I could!"

The policeman dropped Shirley's arm and turned to Bill's grandmother. "You're her mother?"

"No, I'm *his* grandmother," she said, nodding to Bill. "And it's just an oatcake."

"You're not in the same family?"

"No, she's my grandson's little friend."

The policeman pressed a button on the side of his gas mask. "I'm gonna need a car here." To Bill's grandmother, he said, "Ma'am, there's no mixed eating. And there's no eating outside."

Her face took on a scowl that Bill had never seen before. It was a look of disgust he would come to identify with later in his life, but then, as a boy, it terrified him. His grandmother's face hardly changed in any outward sense, nothing beyond her brow furrowing and the corners of her mouth dropping down. But the friendly woman he knew was gone, if only temporarily. The very skin of her grew as cold and unforgiving as stone.

"You're a pig, and you make us live as pigs. Stuck inside and cooped up. No *mixed* eating? Do you know what you sound like? In my day? How dare you!"

"Ma'am, please, you can't be here. And I'm going to have to take the food."

Bill's grandmother stood up. She'd taken her shoes off and stood barefoot on top of the blanket, the plastic grass jabbing into her feet. She was tired, confused, and she missed her husband as if it were the first time. He had died three years ago and was the last person she knew who remembered how things used to be, before the heat, before the health regulations, before police officers and soldiers permanently hid their faces behind gas masks, in the final years before the world became legislatively unfriendly. She missed him so much that she could almost feel him become undead, as though her rage were powerful enough to summon him back to life. She could feel him with her, his reassuring warmth, his zest for life, a kind of enthusiasm that few were permitted to exercise anymore. Intoxicated by that feeling, she threw the oatcakes at the officer. Then she picked up her shoes. She threw one at him. Before she could throw the other, Bill had snatched it from her hand and thrown it for her. Shirley ran away, and in the commotion, no one noticed that she'd picked up an oatcake off the ground and taken it with her.

Bill and his grandmother went to jail that night, and because it was Friday, they stayed in for the whole weekend. The quality of the food was decent, and they ate well, and because they were family, they were allowed to eat together.

The next time Bill saw Shirley, she was wearing the toy ring with the plastic garnet. Her front tooth was chipped, but it didn't stay that way, because there was a dentist in the area who gave everyone in the district a reduced price.

POPE AND HUME

The wolfdog was a male yearling, and the wild man took Pope to visit him every day.

Though his groans, yelps, and calls sounded different to Pope, there was still a trace of wild in them. There was nothing so disturbing in his noises like the animals in the dog park, or the poor caged creatures at the kennel. Each day, in the cool of the morning, the wild man retrieved Pope from his lonely cage and gave him some dried meat. The feeling of being led was utterly foreign to Pope, but what was more unnatural was being alone in a cage. He welcomed the sight of the wild man, his smell, and the paces they took together each day.

For a wolf out of step with the natural world, the requirement for a pack was stripped down to the most basic element: the mutuality of being.

The yearling was quick to bow to Pope's dominance, though it initially surprised Pope. Next to his brother, it did not appear he would be best suited for the role of an alpha. While his mother was alive, she was the pack leader, and Pope, as the smaller of the two pups, was content in the role of beta. It was assumed that his larger brother would find a mate and form a pack, and Pope would follow along as they acquired more members.

The beta wolf played an important function in the structure of the pack. He supported his alpha in his leadership duties, helped raise the pups, and encouraged and kept in line lower-level members of the pack. He helped coordinate hunts, tracking, distracting, and weakening large prey, setting the stage for the alpha to deliver the terminal, suffocating bite.

Pope played this role to a minor degree in his family pack, but after being orphaned, he fell into step with the only role available to him: that of a lone wolf, specifically, a lone alpha. He was prepared to set out as a full-grown wolf in a pack of his own creation. In the time he spent tracing up the Rockies, first with his family pack, and then alone, and as the wolf calls grew scarce, he doubted that would become a reality.

Now he had wandered into another reality, among creatures that made no sense to him. The dog breeds he saw, the French bulldogs, poodles, terriers, shepherds, looked like deformities of nature. They were strange, and he cringed at their weird utterances, awkward gaits, high-pitched yelps, and labored breathing. Among them all, the wolfdog stood out the most clearly, because he was most like Pope. It was a question of survival, and left with no other choice, Pope used his time with the wolfdog to both teach and learn a new language, and in that way, create a new language of their own.

Immediately upon each visit, when Pope entered the enclosure, he would pull up his lip and growl until the wolfdog submitted. He would come and lick Pope's muzzle, and Pope's growl eventually quieted. Pope made chattering sounds, huffed air, and let the wolfdog's nose touch his, and this was the way he allowed the wolfdog to greet him. The wolfdog would whimper and whine, letting Pope take his muzzle in his mouth. This was how they said hello.

Ppp – hhohh – pp - hahh, said Pope.

Mmm – heeww – mm – hehh

Hmm – eww – mm – haah

Hh – eww – mm, said the wolfdog.

And just as Pope is called Pope because of his particular combination of utterances and physical habits, the wolfdog developed a signature sound, something which could be used to mark his existence, to place his experience within a being. Out of the sound of him comes a name, out of *hh – eww – mm,* Hume emerges.

The wild man brought small game carcasses for them to feed on, and through the ritual of eating, Pope's dominance was further established. He bared his teeth and growled when Hume got too close, so he crawled on his belly toward the food and didn't begin eating until Pope licked his lips and turned his head away. And then, only very cautiously. Pope listened to Hume chomping at flesh, the meat, sinew, and bones ripping and snapping. This was the only sound the wolfdog made that sounded truly wild at all.

It was on one afternoon in April when the ground roasted from the taunting summer sun, as Pope and Hume sprawled themselves on the cold cement under the shadow of a tree, that the wild man never came to take Pope back to his cage.

It was the following morning, as Pope and Hume woke in the lingering mildness of the night's air when something other than aloneness began to take shape.

THE WORLD OF MEN BEHIND

Bill

It was an unseasonably cool morning when the clouds obscured the sun just a little longer as it came over the edge of the valley, when Bill decided to open the gate for the final time to what had become the wolf enclosure. An early summer virus had spread through a nearby town, and nearly all the men who worked at the kennel caught it. The men called it the *summer ills*, and the women called it seasonal allergies. In truth, as the season progressed, fewer and fewer people could go outside without experiencing intense respiratory inflammation.

The summer produced intense blooms over the remaining countryside, and pollen hung thick in the air like a summer snow. When Bill was a boy, the most common cause of summer death was due to the intense heat that began as early as March. By the time he was a teenager, death from anaphylaxis became another common cause. At first, Bill counted himself as one of the lucky ones, but as more began to die, and those who didn't die isolated themselves, he didn't count himself anything but lonely.

He hadn't brought a lead with him. Instead of stepping into the wolf enclosure, he opened the gate and stepped ten paces toward the edge of the kennel compound, near another gate which led into a wood. He patted his leg, and the wolfdog, being the more *dog* among them, trotted anxiously after Bill. The wolfdog was not quite a pet, but he was not wild either, and Bill took advantage of this mixture to form an attachment, one that was typical in the world of men, but impossible in the wild. It was friendly and submissive. Regarding the wolf, Bill didn't know what to expect just yet, and he was prepared to be patient.

In the wolf, the nature of profound vicious independence was dominant. When Bill had opened the gate, the wolf was curled up, asleep, his head resting on his paws. At least, he *appeared* asleep, and Bill initially believed the charade. But then he saw one of the wolf's eyes open, and quickly wink closed again. Then he did the same with his other eye. It didn't open fully, but Bill caught a glimpse of the piercing yellow iris. The wolf's ears were upright, focused, and unmoving to the human eye. His body was completely still, his bushy tail wrapped lazily around his hindquarters, continuing to play as though he were asleep. But he saw Bill watching him, he must have. Bill knew that the wolf *knew* that Bill knew it wasn't asleep, and yet he carried on, winking one eye open, and then the other. For a moment, it was playful, like a wolf pup playing with its parent. Then the wolf closed his eyes and kept them shut.

The wolf was in the world of men, but not *of* it, and Bill thought he could see, behind each wink, and even now with his eyes closed, that the wolf winced at the sight of the metal fences, as though they stung and cut into his flesh like actual bindings. Maybe he was winking out of playfulness, or maybe it was to avoid having to see too much of where he lived. But the fence was open, and the wolf would have to see that sometime.

Of course, he already did.

Bill adjusted the Stetson on his head, pushing back in vain the curly hair which refused to stay tucked behind his ear, hoisted his rifle strap over his shoulder, and headed out into the wood. The wolfdog followed a few paces behind, cautious as a wolf yet curious and excited as a dog.

The woods outside were thick with understory, and morning dew still sat on the long, arching leaves and bristly bushes. Plants grew strangely from the intense heat and short winters. There was once an unspoken cycle, a time of blossom and bloom followed by wilt and decay. A sacrifice to nature's exuberance, to reimagine death into something else. But the cycle lost its foothold, and plants remained alive and thriving, burning long after their expiration date. Oversized leaves yellowed at the tips, and the green center throbbed like a fire in the forest that never went out.

Bill swatted dandelion tufts away from his face, but he didn't sneeze. He wasn't necessarily stronger, just more ready to adapt to the surge of the natural world. Where others had diminished and succumbed to nature's overwhelming force, it had been Bill's physiological inclination to thrive in this environment. He had grown thick against the sun and heat, like a gourd, perhaps inside and out. Things surrounded him differently, his senses and sensitivities refreshed and evolved like a new kind of animal, borne out of changed ecological conditions. The environment was not sub-optimal or treacherous to any greater degree than it once was at various moments in history. It simply required a new adaptation.

Bill could hear the padding of his own footsteps as they rustled through the brush.

Duhh – auw – psshh – mm – pff.

Buhh – oamm – sshh – mm – pp.

The sounds bounced off the boundaries of his own skull, interrupted only by the rhythm of his breath, steadily in and out through his nostrils, the little hairs being pulled and pushed by the flow of air. He wondered if the sounds of his aliveness, the clomping of his boots, the precise note of his breath, and all the other little sounds were more his truer name than *Bill* ever had been. But then he forgot that thought, just as soon as he'd had it, and walked on, leaving the kennel and the world of men behind him.

Pope

From the sleeping nest he'd made the previous night, Pope watched the wild man approach the enclosure, and even though he'd seen him in this exact context before and knew there was nothing to fear...

...with a human, he remained vigilant.

Pope held his position, curled up and closed his eyes, determined to make Bill believe he was asleep. He opened one eye. Only a little. Carefully. Quickly. Then shut both tightly. The wild man had been on his left foot, his right foot sailing up just slightly, grazing the tops of the grass blades. Breeze caught his mane, lifting his bushy hair into the wind of his stride. His arms swung heavily; his hands were pendulous. Pope opened one eye, closed it, then another, and closed it, and in this way, he watched the wild man approach, learning the tiny pieces of his movements. He kept his eyes closed and listened. He felt the slight shaking of the ground with each step. He heard his breath sucking in through his nose and forced out over a wet tongue, sending out the aromatics of an acidic mouth still digesting breakfast.

Pope didn't know the word *wild,* but that's exactly what this man was. He smelled different from other humans. He reeked of food and pheromones in a way that only animals did. His hair grew in thick, bushy tufts, and he always seemed on the verge of being engulfed by it. His arms swung like tree trunks – if a tree could uproot itself and walk through the forest, that's what it would sound like: the thumping of his gait, the rustling of the underbrush as he moved, the crack of fallen branches under wide feet, the *whoosh* from the displacement of the air encircling him.

Though Pope had had limited contact with human beings, this man felt familiar to him in a basic and primal way. But that didn't mean he didn't fear him. There was something untethered in him, and Pope wasn't sure if it was inborn or the product of a brutal, unforgiving world. He was *animal.* He was a wild man, and if provoked, wild things are lethal.

Pope opened his eyes just as the wild man and Hume disappeared into the forest. He sat up and shook his body, morning mist raining off his black coat. He licked his lips and settled. He was hungry, but not in the way he'd been when he first arrived at the kennel. The skin on his torso no longer clung quite so desperately to his ribcage, and his coat was a little fuller. He had regained just enough strength for the memory of painful hunger to have faded slightly. He pulled himself out of his position in the corner of the enclosure and edged cautiously toward the woods, the fragrance of freedom beckoning him.

Hume trotted back and flashed Pope a look of engagement. His puppy-like eyes were pools of hopefulness: An excitement to be somewhere other than the kennel, and a longing for Pope to follow. He whined and swished his tail to make his desires clear. Padding the ground in a slow walk and then speeding up to a trot, Pope caught up to Hume, who tucked his tail until Pope licked him, like a brother.

The sun had just started to come up over the valley ridge, illuminating the wild man from behind. His hair was overgrown, sticking out from the sides of his Stetson, obscuring any shape of a human head. At the front of the tiny pack, he was like a totem, a remnant of a history lost, and an emblem for something new to take its place.

From somewhere deep in the woods came several high-pitched chirping sounds, followed by a long, roaring screech, and Pope froze, his ears perked forward in attention. There was a small elk family nearby. He knew he could bolt and run away, leaving his alien captors behind, speeding faster and farther. Suddenly, his mind driven purely by primordial instinct, the wild man and Hume lost the roles and registers they had grown into and became only organisms of shape and breath, threatening and strange in their demeanor.

Pope listened for the sound and when he heard it, he broke into a sprint, feeling a lightness from the distance expanding between him, Hume, and the wild man, like a heavy dream fading with the relief of consciousness.

NO LOUDER THAN AN ECHO

The sun was coming up over the edge of the valley, and though the morning air was still cool, Bill could feel the heat of the day ahead.

It was early in the year, and the temperature probably wouldn't go much above 35 Celsius, but direct sunlight could feel ten degrees hotter. Right now, it was filtered through the lattice of the forest, and it flashed in Bill's eyes with each step.

Finding work as a ranger in Yellowstone had been one of the great thrills of his life. In watching it burn, he knew he was watching a part of the Earth vanish forever. He'd read enough history of the past hundred years to know what would happen next: The fires would go out, and the ground would settle. The arid climate would frighten off new growth, and seeds dropped by passing birds and winds would dry and turn to dust. There would be no smell, sound, or life, just a heat haze wavering off the cracked earth.

And then people would come with cranes and trucks filled with wire, bricks, concrete, and plumbing. A contained settlement would be built with homes, hospitals, grocery stores, greenhouses, fish farms, clothing stores, and everything else a society might need to survive. Black roads, cutting through the once lush hillsides, passing by dried-up geysers, would be paved and connected directly into the enormous settlement compounds. There would be schools too, and in those schools the children would be taught how there used to be national parks, one of which was called Yellowstone National Territory, and it used to be somewhere near the place they now called home.

With modern building techniques, that kind of transformation could very well happen within a decade of The Great Fire. Bill could have contacted a local building company to get in early, as the other rangers did. After all, he was out of work, just like them. But even though he grew up in the concrete of the outskirts of New York City, the woods were too important to him. Watching their demise had been painful enough, and he couldn't bear to contribute to the final casket closure. He'd made his way north, driving along the Rockies, up into Alaska, and then further into the Yukon, one of the last untouched natural places in North America, and found work at the Beaver Spring dog kennel.

The sound of the wolf running was no louder than a muffled echo, but it stood out in contrast to the calmness of the woods. Less than fifteen minutes had passed since Bill had opened the gate and walked away from the kennel grounds, and the wolf had been asleep. At least, he appeared asleep. Bill turned just in time to see a black wolf galloping towards him, mouth open, panting like a dog, but with eyes that pierced in a way that no dog's ever could. He looked frightening, and Bill wondered if his idea to leave the kennel, to take the opportunity when everyone was out sick and attempt to rehome this wolf, had been wise.

He moved his fingers around his gun, mostly in an attempt to brace himself. His grip tightened as the wolf approached, moving through the air as if in slow motion. It was more than just the startling series of thuds that he'd heard a moment earlier. It was as though a vacuum had sucked out all other sounds, and the wolf tore through that stillness.

Time moved differently for a moment. Each second passed deliberately, forming a visible outline that became sharper and more defined. The air changed, sweeping in from a fresh direction. It came from another stratospheric place, filtering out stagnation, changing the gaseous composition, and lowering the temperature slightly, but noticeably. What Bill breathed in, no one had breathed before.

His eyes were locked with the wolf's, and he heard the panting, the in and out of the breath against fangs and a wet tongue. He heard the *papping* sound of paw pads against the earth, the grittiness of the dirt, the crunching of leaves and twigs. He heard the shaking of loose skin against muscle and bone, and the rustling sound of the wolf's midnight-colored fur as it shook back and forth with each stride.

Ppp – Hahhh – Ppp – Uhh
Fsshhh – huupp
Pepp – Ohh – P – Ehh
P – Oh – P
Sshhh – whuupp

There was a range of sounds, and within them was a pattern that Bill could just barely make out. It was like trying to remember the words to a song, just out of memory's reach. There was a rhythm, something repeated, like a message from the wolf. He could see it in the particular stride, the unique composure, the way the wolf's paws hit the ground, the back left a little before the front right, and so on. It was a message that Bill heard but couldn't interpret.

Fsshhh – huupp – puh – puh
Pepp – Ohh – P – Ehh
Huup – puh – puh
Ppp – Oh – Pphh

The wolf swerved off in another direction and vanished into the green, and the clock in Bill's head returned to ticking as normal. The wolfdog whined and danced on the spot, unsure of what to do.

"Shh," said Bill. "Alright there, boy." He put his hand out, and the wolfdog came over and sniffed it, distractedly. He whined, and his face, although handsome, in comparison to the wolf, looked almost like a toy, his young, yellowish eyes set in brown/grey fur. His snout and jaw, though fierce, showed none of the wolf's unbridled ferociousness. He was like a copy, if a human tried to imitate a wolf, not having a full grasp of what they were trying to produce.

Bill heard several animal calls from somewhere deeper in the woods. A series of chirping sounds and then a chilling screech that almost took physical form, pressing against his eardrums. Bill wasn't sure what the calls belonged to, but it was something very large, and judging from the wolf's speed, one thing was certain:

A hunt had begun.

Bill set off toward the calls with the wolfdog leading the way, following the wolf's scent. He wondered if the animal had run off for good and if he'd ever see it again. A longing stirred in Bill, a sadness that he might never get to know this creature in its true environment, that his time with wolves had burned up in the Fire at Yellowstone. But something told him to keep going. If he'd learned one thing about wolves, it was how similar to humans they were. Like people, wolves needed a community. They couldn't survive on their own. But it was specifically the company of other wolves that they needed. Bill wondered if the wolf had run toward possible prey, or away from him...

"We need a name for you, boy," Bill mumbled, unsure if he was talking to himself or the wolfdog. It was the second time he'd called him *boy*, and the wolfdog turned his head when he did. "Gotta make sure you come when I call."

THE PACK EMERGES

Pope

Pope belly-crawled to the edge of a clearing, hidden by taller grasses. Eyes focused, ears pinned back, he watched as a cow elk and her two calves grazed by a creek. He had hoped to find a calf alone, as it would be easier to take down by himself. A whole family was more than he could handle alone, and if the cow was here, the bull was surely nearby, and a bull would rip him apart. He'd seen it happen as a pup, after the migration north but before the land dried up so much that elk couldn't even graze.

The sight of the elk and the odor of their urine and musk in the breeze stoked Pope's adrenaline, as well as his fear. But he was hungry for freshly killed meat, and more than that, he was hungry to do the killing himself. He hadn't hunted properly since his mother and brother had been struck down by the violence of distemper. A hunt wasn't just about the food; it was about the group in which it was executed. It was about coming together for a common cause, a celebration of survival, another day won. And it was about knowing that he was exactly where he belonged.

In the absence of community and a sense of membership, desire is given no direction. It becomes whittled down to its most primary essence, and in Pope's case, the core of that was: to endure. Risky decisions are made when a wolf's impulse to persevere is done for himself alone, without the context of a role and the status of a pack. As his mouth watered and his nostrils twitched, scenarios ran through his mind about how he might isolate one of the calves. It would be the only way he could reasonably hope for a successful kill – one in which he prevailed with minimal injury.

He heard rustling sounds behind him, and, forgetting all else, immediately took it as a threat.

Something was coming to take his prey, and he had to defend his position.

He felt attacked on all sides and crouched down even lower, flattening himself as much as possible to avoid being seen. But then, like with a memory that comes back in thin shades of color, the reality of the past month returned to his mind. There had been a man, a different sort of man, a man with a smell he'd recognized, a man with something *wild* in him. Who had freed him or taken him captive – that remained to be discovered. And there was an animal that looked like a wolf but wasn't. It had whined and whimpered and licked Pope's muzzle. It had responded to Pope's dominance and learned to trust him.

Mmm – heeww – mm – heeh

Hh – eww – mm

Pope heard Hume's whine and immediately got up and trotted back into the forest. This was not an ambush by an unknown threat; this was the arrival of his pack. Not like any pack he'd seen or been a part of, but it would have to do, as there was no other way to hunt the elk.

Pope found Hume in the brush and blocked his way. Larger than Hume, he bristled his fur for effect, curled his upper lip, and growled. Hume quieted his whine, tucked his tail between his legs, and sank to the ground. Pope turned back to face the direction of the clearing with the elk, and Hume came up alongside Pope and sat down next to him, to indicate that he would submit and go where he was told.

Bill

"Boy!" shouted Bill. "Where'd he run off to..."

Bill found the wolfdog sitting next to the wolf, who towered over him. Both were alert, sniffing something in the air. Bill cocked his rifle and at the sound of the *click clock,* the wolf turned his head slightly and growled.

Bill felt the wolf's growl in his stomach, and it reverberated up into his throat. The wolf was on edge, and the sound of the metal made things worse. He put the safety back on and dropped the gun, letting it swing at his side by the shoulder strap.

"Alright, it's ok b—"

He started to call the wolf *Boy,* but he realized he'd already started calling the wolfdog *boy.* They couldn't both be *Boy.* He wasn't even sure if the wolf would ever recognize a name if he gave him one. The wolves at Yellowstone had names, but that was just for the researchers and rangers to be able to keep track of them within the park, to try and learn pack dynamics, and to know which wolves died, when their time came.

There was only one time he'd ever given a wolf a name, but that was later.

He'd often wondered if wolves had names for each other, but that wasn't anything a human could confirm.

"Alright, wolf. It's alright." Against every instinct of self-protection, Bill dropped his hands to his sides, and the wolf stopped growling. He could see, though, from his profile, that he continued watching Bill and continued curling his upper lip as he did.

A breeze swept through where they stood, rustling the brush and the trees, and the wolf got up on all four feet. Boy did, too, and Bill watched as they set off together into the thick brush that bordered the meadow. It wasn't a trot or a run, and it wasn't a wander. It was a stalk. There was purpose in their gait; they knew where they were going. Bill followed close behind. He was quiet, but it was out of respect rather than secrecy. He knew there was no concealing his presence, least of all from the wolf.

That he was allowed to follow at all was a gift.

On another edge of the clearing, still protected by the density of the thicket and bramble, the wolf dropped to the ground and flattened his ears against his head. Boy did the same thing. Further out in the field, the ground sloped gently down to a creek, and next to it grazed an elk family, a cow and her two calves. Next to the creek, the forest trees rocked from the low, concentrated weight of a bull elk as it emerged into the clearing. The call Bill had heard earlier came again: A sky-shattering screech followed by some guttural honking noises. The bull elk emerged from the woods with tall, flesh-ripping antlers and joined his family by the creek.

The wolf stayed motionless, and Boy took that as his cue, and so did Bill, and no one moved.

TOWARD THE FURY

When Bill was twelve, he and Shirley ran away for two days. Standing next to her at the mouth of an enormous meadow, Bill tried to contain his startled response when Shirley's hand brushed his. He hoped he'd caught it. He hoped it was one of those imperceptible jumps, only noticed by the one whose body it inhabits. They stood together on the crest of the hill, overlooking a space so large that it was difficult for their eyes to adjust to the depth. It was larger than anything one could reasonably get to from Queens, and indeed, how far they'd traveled was unreasonable for their age and the time of year.

At one time in history, it might have looked like two love-sick teenagers on a quest to carve out their own space in the world. In this meadow, they had found a last remnant of something wild, stubbornly resisting the influence of an overwhelmingly man-made earth, and they had found it together. Bill's fingers wiggled, hoping again to haphazardly catch Shirley's still hovering in the air next to his, but she had moved too far away.

Shirley's birthday was on February 29th, and the automatic lock-ins started every year on March 1st. But every leap year, the world stayed open one day longer, and Bill and Shirley had twenty-four extra hours to enjoy open spaces, as open as one could find. The year of Shirley's thirteenth birthday, she went with her parents on a special camping trip in January and invited Bill to come along. They packed up their electric car and drove to the Mohonk Preserve, just outside the New Paltz residential zone. Temperatures at this time of year were just beginning to rise, but this time it was unusually warm.

By 2030, winter had already shortened to a degree that the World Climate Foundation (an organization comprising parts of the defunct World Health Organization and northern states of the former European Union) declared winter to be a *sub-season*. The northern territories of the United States decided to institute mandatory lockdowns for certain seasons and times of the day. Initially, the lockdowns happened just at the height of the summer months, in July and August. But as the average summertime death rate climbed along with the soaring temperatures, the lockdowns were extended, eventually covering all months except November, December, January, and February. Spring and autumn had effectively vanished, and summer stretched into one long undulating season. Winter was brief and often began with a critical drop in temperature and subsequent hailstorms and blizzards.

Bill and Shirley were eleven months apart in age, and they often celebrated their birthdays together. Bill's birthday was at the end of January, and he was used to celebrating his at home, as the weather was rarely stable enough to plan a camping trip. January could be a strange month of transition, ranging from uncomfortable heat spikes to freezing blizzards. The year Shirley turned thirteen, the newspapers wrote of the unusually temperate weather, calling it "a new spring".

Bill and Shirley had left the campsite just after breakfast, promising her parents they were only going on a short walk. The low-lying morning sun shimmered off the granite walls that enclosed a leafless forest, the glint of the shine stinging their eyes as they wandered. Climbing uphill in the brief early morning chill, Bill could see Shirley's breath puffing around her head as she led the way. She was faster than him, for a time, taller than him, and always bolder than him.

Bill first met Shirley when he was five years old. He'd gotten lost, but not in any real way. Rather, it was in that childish way, the memory of which is filled with far more emotion and gravity than the situation itself. His grandmother had left him at the enclosed playground near their building, just as she did every day at 6:30 in the evening when the doors opened. He'd wandered outside, down the street, and around the corner, and as if the shape of the world had transformed, he was lost. He wandered along the city block as his panic grew, sat down on the ground, and began to cry, an uninhibited wailing cry.

A shoe met his.

Paapppf.

He looked up and saw Shirley: A yellow sundress and a brown hat, pale skin, and a disappointed squint on her face.

"Stop that." She turned to walk away, fishing him out of his despondency with each step. "Come on."

Driven purely by instinct, he obeyed.

And now she was leading the way again, and he was following, because everywhere Shirley was, was better. With her, no adventure was too scary, nor any discovery too impossible. Shirley brought the world to life for Bill, and to get his experiences purely from books would never again be enough for him. Wherever she went, looking dead ahead with intensity and charged with energy, he would always follow, even if it meant watching her back. It was the best, most exciting back he had ever known.

The two ascended at a steady pace until the ground leveled out. The woods then took on a different form, in that unexpected and unnamed way that only a quiet wood can. The path dipped back down, the trees grew taller, and the view of the granite walls surrounding the valley was blocked out. Bill inhaled and felt the air in his nose change. It seemed to take on a new note of freshness, as though it had been distilled, newly borne from the surrounding trees, and never breathed before.

Bill saw Shirley's pace slow, and for the first time in a long time, for it was not particularly in her nature, she turned her head back, taking her eyes off the path ahead, and smiled at him. Her nostrils flared slightly, and it was as if the air had enlivened something in her. The chatter of the springtime birds soared as well, as though they were not simply revived as usual from the all too short winter or the previous night, but newly animated by the exceptional air that seemed to have descended on this bit of wood. The path thinned and curved to the left, a little back to the right, and just as it seemed to disappear altogether, the forest closing in, the trees simply ended. Bill and Shirley found themselves at the mouth of a gasping meadow.

Something began moving toward them. At first, it was far enough away not to feel threatening. The meadow was so large that Bill and Shirley initially had no concept of the distance. Whatever it was they saw could have been very close but also very small. Or it could have been far away. Their eyes struggled to adjust, but as soon as they did, each felt their breath catch in their throats.

Bill reached out for Shirley's hand. He wanted her to turn and grab him, protect him, run them back to the concrete city where all the grass was fake, and everything was safe and known. His eyes were locked on the thing in the meadow as it grew larger, and he stumbled as his hand reached to where he thought Shirley was, panicking to find that she was not. Bill shook his eyes free and found the back of Shirley's head, her straight, dark brown hair wisping ever so slightly in the wind, as she walked toward the thing, which was slowly starting to look more like a large, galloping, black wolfdog.

The dog's tongue flapped out of its mouth wildly as it bounded in the direction of Bill and Shirley. It was hard to know at first who the dog was running toward, but with each sailing stride, and as Shirley progressed farther into the meadow, the distance between her and Bill growing, it became clear: The dog had picked Shirley. In her almost destructive adventurousness, she reached her hand out, not knowing if it would be licked or bitten, and not caring too much, so long as the bite wasn't very serious. Bill's heart fluttered as he watched the dog choose Shirley over him, and it wasn't in anticipation, nor in jealousy, but in awe. Shirley was special to him in a way he couldn't fully explain, and in watching the scene with Shirley and the dog unfold, it was as if nature were explaining it for him.

The dog licked Shirley's hand, then her wrist, and then her forearm. Shirley crouched down lower and lower until she was sitting on the ground, allowing her face to be covered with saliva as the dog joyfully flapped its tongue all over her. Her giggle was like a birdcall, staccato, high-pitched, and gleeful. Bill felt it puncture the air around him, causing his own diaphragm to spasm, and he laughed, silently with a sharp exhale.

He watched as Shirley flopped back on the grass, rolling with the wolfdog in play, both their tongues flashing in delight. Shirley shot Bill a look of utter splendor, once again a smile flashing on her usually serious face, her green eyes gleaming with flecks of yellow. She was glad he was there, and she watched whatever trepidation Bill was feeling recede, the certainty of *her* settling him, and his trust, in turn, settling her.

"STOP!"

One thing that happened, as domesticated dogs were continually bred for city life, is that they lost some essential genes, the absence of which led to the development of a particular syndrome. On the outside, the main symptom that presented was excessive friendliness, and most humans not only had no problem with this but welcomed the development. Humans lived in closer proximity than ever before. Despite this, a strange thing happened: people felt farther apart. Communication switched from the verbal to the digital, doors locked, germs mutated, and most families became very insular.

A few remnants of what could be considered an old-fashioned lifestyle remained, and one of those was the daily dog walk. Particularly during the long summer months, after the doors unlocked, a handful of people would stroll around a given neighborhood, a toy poodle, dachshund, or Scottish terrier on the end of a leash, and relish the one chance they had that day to talk to another person face to face. Dogs were bred specifically for this, to be friendly and open to anyone; there was no need or desire for the trait of territorialism. But this over-breeding also made them weak and susceptible to viruses. City dogs were thought to be safe, so long as they, as well as their owners, stayed away from all contact with wild dogs, which were considered a threat by virtue of being free of human interference. The more humans sought to conquer the natural world, the farther out of reach it became.

As Shirley's father sprinted toward them, he didn't see what Bill saw. He didn't see Shirley's unusually joyful face and was too far out of earshot to hear her giggle. He didn't see Bill's tensed shoulders relax at the sight of her and the wolfdog playing, sensing that despite what he'd heard about dogs in nature, they were not as dangerous as people thought. Bill had never seen a dog this large before and didn't know where it came from, but if Shirley was unafraid, then there was nothing to fear.

But just as Shirley's father couldn't see the situation clearly, and couldn't hear Bill's thoughts, Bill couldn't know the growing panic her father felt. He could see enough to know that Shirley was being covered in an unknown dog's saliva, being saturated with germs she could potentially pass on to their Yorkie at home, and to the other dogs it played with. The risks were numerous, including parasites, flu, parvo, and distemper variants. That it was unexpectedly friendly indicated that it could have the inbred syndrome, but this didn't exempt the dog from being a carrier of disease. The dog was large – too large for a city dog. It was alone. There was no possibility that it was a pet from the nearby residential zone. Her father sped across the meadow from another entry point, furiously hoping to intersect Shirley and the strange dog.

And then Bill and Shirley ran away. Maybe it was the air they had passed through in the woods just before they'd reached the meadow. Maybe it was the security Shirley observed in Bill, developing before her eyes, in tandem with her own, the two building off each other. Or maybe it was the fact that she was days away from turning thirteen, an age when most children start to get ideas separate from those of their parents. Of whatever it was that prompted Shirley to stand up and run, Bill was never certain. But just as he'd followed her as a lost child, and just as he'd gone along with every game she'd suggested when they were little, playing together in the enclosed neighborhood playground, and just as he'd come nervously yet excitedly on this camping trip – he held her hand tightly when she grabbed him, and he ran with her.

They sprinted into the meadow, fists holding tight, fighting the urge to let go because of their uncoordinated gaits. The wolfdog ran alongside them, and Bill felt a surge of elation rise up from his stomach and burst behind his eyes: He felt part of a pack, though it wasn't a word he'd know or understand for many years to come. Shirley was the alpha, Bill was her beta, and the wolfdog was their newest member, however temporary. Shirley pulled his hand, and the group veered out of the meadow, away from her father, and into the thicket. Once inside, they dropped their hands to run more stealthily through the tightly knit trees. Bill never lost sight of Shirley, although the wolfdog eventually vanished from sight, seemingly swallowed up by the woods.

Bill and Shirley wandered through the forest for two days. They didn't know how to camp, but they did it anyway, however poorly. Bill created makeshift shelters, which fell, and the two collected berries, which made them vomit. They didn't know how to dig holes for their waste, and they clung tightly to each other at night because they didn't know how to build a fire. In the afternoon, they reached a clearing, but the sun was so fierce on their skin, they stayed hidden in the thicket. On the second day, they awoke to the sound of a helicopter and ran again, this time toward the fury.

THE SCREECH OF A BULL ELK

Pope

Pope's eyes vibrated from the blinding shriek of the bull elk's bugle.

The heat of the day was only just beginning to rise in the shade of the tree, but in the open meadow, the smell of the elk family baked in the sun. The stench of urine, musk, milky teats, and oily sebum intoxicated Pope. Surrounding the elk, the sun glinted off the textured surface of the grass, shining like a billion needle points, fumes of hot earth rising off them. His muscles clenched with the desire to chase, capture, and sink his teeth into pulsating, living flesh. He sank low in the grass before the elk could spot him and waited.

More than patience, of which a wolf hunt requires a great deal, it involves a change in the quality of perception. While watching the elk, it was as though Pope's normally heightened senses expanded, rendering his entire body a cavernous receptor. Reality took on a sandpapery quality of sharpness and intensity. The way each animal chewed the grass, the squidgy crunch of the blades in their mouth, the sound of gritty dirt beneath their feet, the leaves batting each other as the warm wind swept in upward curves, and the increasing smell of hot earth – There was a lot to pay attention to.

Pope stalked the elk family for nearly six hours as they grazed the field. These were not like the elk he remembered from his days as a pup in Yellowstone. He remembered watching his mother and other older pack members stalking their prey on the dusty, meager lands. All they had to do was trot after them for a while, and the herd would become tired. Those elk were starved – easy prey to catch, yet hardly enough to feed a pack. The pack members responsible for distracting and delivering weakening bites to sinewy hind quarters had an easy job as they prepared the weakest elk for the brute force of the final, jugular-crushing jaw clamp from the alpha.

But the elk family Pope saw now, in these lusher woods, alive with birdcalls and the prickly sounds of nature blooming into early summer fullness, were pungent with good health and vigor. Their brown fur shone in the sunlight, and though the calves meandered only several long strides from him, he knew a kill would not come easily.

Hume waited behind Pope, dutifully and patiently. He watched Pope more than the elk, waiting for a sign to act. Pope's ears were tucked back, so Hume did the same. Pope was perfectly still, so Hume copied him.

At first, it was a blind imitation, very much like a pup with its parent. But then Hume began to see more under the surface of Pope, down to his tendons and the way his fur flinched in sync with various changes in the elk family. A snuff or a grunt, and Pope's muscles would shift, moving his head only slightly more than imperceptibly. Hume clenched his body at the horrifying screech of the elk's bugle, but he noticed that Pope froze, as though he turned into inanimate organic matter, just for a moment. He listened for Pope's breath and took in the smell of his feral hyper-focus. Pope paid no attention to Hume, and Hume now recognized that more than a collection of sounds to which he learned to respond, more than a trot behind a lumbering two-legged creature followed by a submissive lick on the hand, this was the most trusting, most intimate form of leadership.

What happened next, happened fast.

One of the elk calves had wandered away from its family, leaving it isolated. The bull elk was on the other side of the clearing, leaving this moment open. Pope stood up and, after a brief pause, began to walk slowly into the clearing. He knew the elk were somewhat aware of his presence, but not that he was a threat, or they would have left the area. He was a lone wolf, and because of that, not presumed lethal.

But he was not alone. He could summon Hume at any moment, and together they would chase the elk calf until it was far away from its family and bring it down. This would be their first stalk together, their first chase, their first kill, their first true meal as an emerging pack. Pope glanced back at Hume quickly, long enough to make eye contact, to signal that it was time to run. Hume stood up and followed Pope toward the calf, who had already begun to look nervous, edging toward the woods.

A shot rang out, so stunning that it seemed to convulse the entire scene.

The calf honked a piercingly high-pitched sound of pain. The ground shook as the bull elk screeched and barreled in Pope and Hume's direction. Turning to sprint into the woods, Pope saw that there was already a figure running ahead of him. It was the wild man, but now there seemed little that was wild about him.

With Hume close behind, Pope ran away from the elk and toward a man who now seemed more like a boy. Before his eyes, Pope watched him inexplicably change in size. He began to shrink, his head staying large, covered in bushy hair, and his body seemed tiny and weak, almost unable to hold the weight of its large, bulbous head, bobbing with each stride.

It was not a man anymore, but an insolent, inattentive, and useless creature, and Pope felt himself huge in comparison. It had called the attention of the bull elk, destroying Pope's opportunity to isolate the calf in a chase. Even though the elk's bugles grew softer in intensity as Pope ran, he sprinted through the trees as though he were chasing something. His breath was hot with rage toward this tiny creature, dodging and weaving his way through the forest. Pope's eyes sharpened, and the intention of his sprint turned from one of fleeing to one of pursuing. The wild man was gone, and Pope could eat this creature in a single bite if given the chance.

He would threaten, but he would not eat, and that is what loyalty looks like.

Bill

At the screech of the bull elk, the wolf had dropped down low in the tall grass and flattened his ears against his head. From behind, his black body was easy to mistake for shadows in the thicket. Boy dropped low at the wolf's side, but also just a little behind. His body was smaller than the wolf's, and he nearly vanished into the grass. Bill lowered himself as quietly as he could but kept his distance. Both heads were trained toward the elk family. The bull elk screeched and bugled.

They watched for a long time. The bull elk quieted down and focused on grazing and minding his family. Bill wasn't a hunter, and after a while, a sense of peace overtook him. A playful breeze danced with the curly hair that bushed out of the sides of his hat. The shade of a large tree provided much-needed coverage from the midday April sun. It was early summer, and the temperatures after noon would creep close to brutal. If they left the kennel permanently and stayed gone, he'd have to find a place for himself before the end of the month, as well as for the wolf and Boy, before the rising temperatures would be deadly for all three of them.

Several hours passed, and everyone kept their places. Bill knew what the wolf was watching for, he knew how wolves stalked their prey. He'd seen this kind of thing at Yellowstone. A wolf hunt could go on for hours and hours, longer than a human's attention could hold. It might be days if they never found a window of opportunity, or if their presence became known and compromised their attack.

But for himself, Bill didn't know anything about hunting. It had become known as an outdated occupation, and like slavery, something people regarded in conversation with comments like *If I had been alive then, I never would have done that*. People didn't eat meat much anymore, not like they did in the earlier part of the 21st century. Back then, veganism was more of a trend, but as the CO2 levels increased and the ice caps melted almost entirely, governments legislated animal farms. Veganism grew to be thought of as ineffective and was replaced by something called Neo-Abolitionism. Many saw it as the natural progression of *ethical veganism*, the surest way for such an ideology to become politicized, and therefore, finally have an influence.

The Neo-Abolitionists felt that the rise of humanity was made largely possible by the enslavement of animals, which many felt had begun with the domestication of the wolf. In man's early days of nomadic life, wolves learned to live with tribes of people. Men took lessons in hunting from the wolf and adopted them into their hunting parties. Upon seeing how similar wolves and humans were – the nurturing of the young, the need for community, and cooperation within a hierarchy toward a larger goal – a mysterious kinship arose. The sound of their howl took up residence in the human psyche as one of the most iconic and elusive symbols of the wild. There is, and has always been, something of the wolf in humans.

But because man's evolution is one of the mind, innovation and change are a part of human expression and development. Wolves may have started out learning to live with humans, but eventually, this cohabitation was forced upon them, developing a new breed of animal: the domesticated dog. The wild nature that helped shape humans as early nomadic hunters was snuffed out in favor of something easier to tame. It was their own wild nature that man wanted to see run free, not the wolf's.

As much progress as he makes, as many innovations of thought and intelligent design, mankind visits a manifold of destruction upon the environment that birthed his very existence.

Agrarianism led to industrialism, and then the final enslavement came: Trapped in camps, denied their natural freedom, man murdered the animals and used their bodies as food. And the food wasn't just to nourish and sustain humanity. Domesticated dogs, genetically engineered for personality and aesthetics, robbed of the drive to stalk, hunt, and kill, sat at man's feet and ate the murdered flesh with him. They grew sad and became stupid, slow, and weak because the animals they ate were sad, stupid, slow, and weak. If one's life span is, at most, a matter of months, locked in a cage and waiting for death, there is probably no other way to be.

It was these slaughterhouses, these animal factories, that played a significant role in damaging the Earth's atmosphere. Massive installments of methane-producing animals caused greenhouse gases to run amok. Governments forced slaughterhouses to drastically reduce their output, and meat grew in cost until it became affordable only to the wealthiest, of which Bill and his family were certainly not. It was around 2050, just as Bill was entering his early teenage years, that the Neo-Abolitionists were formed. It became almost impossible to get a hunting license, and guns were used primarily to stun animals that had ventured into areas they didn't belong, such as small, family-owned Alpaca farms or free-range chicken coops.

Because they had posed a threat to livestock – and therefore, the livelihood of farmers – wolves had been killed almost to the point of extinction, drastically changing the ecosystem and balance of animal populations. A new solution came into force, both for wolves and wolf breeds. That solution was to re-home, not to kill. A hunter deserved to be reacquainted with his natural environment. One animal killing another was the way of nature. A human killing a wild animal for food was considered a crime against the very humanity he was fighting to feed.

But in re-homing, re-educating might become necessary, both for the wolves and humans alike. There were too many unanswered questions because humans had been out of the food chain for far too long. For an animal outside of the food chain, to kill and to murder were the same thing.

Humans had become a negation of their own deep desire to make things better. They just don't agree on what the word *better* means.

~

Bill had been nearly asleep when he startled awake, hearing something rustling nearby.

Feeling safe and unaware of any threat in their vicinity, the elk family had split apart. The bull elk had wandered to one edge of the clearing, and one of the elk calves had wandered in the opposite direction, to an edge closer to where the wolf, Boy, and Bill were lying. The calf was young, isolated, and unprotected. The wolf stood up slowly, and after inching to the very edge of the tall grass, began to walk toward the calf, with Boy following close behind.

What happened next, happened fast.

Bill stumbled to his feet and gripped his rifle. He took the safety off and aimed, taking the elk calf in sight. He crept slowly forward and, noticing his jagged breathing, tried to slow it down to a steady in-and-out. He imagined he was gliding through water, slow and deliberate. He took aim and once the calf was within a suitable range, he exhaled, and shot.

He had never killed an animal before, but somehow, he knew everything had been leading up to this. The carcasses of jackrabbits, raccoons, and deer that he'd given the wolf and Boy when they were back in the kennel had been accidental kills, found on the edge of farmland when they'd roamed too close and been shocked by electric fences. But away from the kennel, they all needed to survive. He'd learned how to forage as a boy, but wolves and dogs were carnivores. Without a pack for them to join, he needed to be more than a forager. He needed to help them survive until they acclimated to this new environment.

Bill was angry but not surprised the bullet missed the calf, who released a high-pitched yelp in fear. The bullet hit a nearby tree. But the louder call rang from the bull, who had Bill in his sights. It was twice his height and carried ten times the weight of even the largest wolf. The ground shook as the enormous animal barreled toward Bill, rocking its bony antlers and screeching in fury.

Bill turned into the forest and ran, hoping the dense trees would make it impossible for the elk to chase him. And he was right, the elk didn't follow. He kept running and heard a few more screeches and barks, and the further he ran, the further away they sounded, vanishing in the vastness of the woods. But he was still aware that he was being chased. He continued running, glancing back in quick movements to see what was behind him.

It was the wolf.

DEAR READER,

There are certain events in life, despite their seeming importance to the greater story of us, that we simply forget.

Sometimes, it's because they don't align with our own vision of who we are and the personal sense of character that we develop over time. We edit the series of events in our lives to blend into a pleasingly coherent story and leave out the parts that contradict or throw wrenches in that tale when we recount it. But, to paraphrase a great thinker of the 20th century: We tend to confuse the actuality of ourselves with the way we would *describe* ourselves to be. Description is very important to human beings. Without it, we hardly believe we exist at all.

I think; therefore, I am?

Or is it, *I am; only thought of as such?*

Other times, we tend to overinflate the importance of certain occurrences because of what we feel they lend to our overarching narrative. There are things we wish to be true about ourselves, so much so that we'll spend more time wishing for them than accepting one of two realities: That we must act to make the wish a truth, or that our wish exceeds what we're capable of accomplishing. But in large part, we are what our minds perceive us to be. To borrow from another great thinker of an entirely different century: Thinking makes it so.

And could anyone say that a thing obtained by wishing it into conception – to be likable, to be worthy, to be on the right side of morality – is any less real than a thing obtained in some visible, earthly way?

Being likable, being worthy, being on the right side of morality – or not – is the same either way. Whether we think we are, or we think we aren't, we're right. Yet still we go on wishing as though we have to prove ourselves wrong.

To return to the subject of remembering or not remembering (sometimes also called forgetting): There's something else that happens in these processes. In either case, the memory degrades. The more a human being consciously recalls something from memory into their active, cognitive space, the more that memory becomes distorted. Over and over again, in their lust to relive something wonderful, people slowly rob themselves of their memories *by the very act of* recollecting them. It's both one of the saddest and the most wonderful truths about human beings. The fact that we degrade our own memories simply by being sentimental, we create a "Schrödinger's cat" version of the truth: The past both exists and does not exist. It's the malleability of it that allows us to truly inhabit our backstories and makes us unreliable storytellers at the same time.

Likewise, when something has been blocked, shut out, erased, stuffed down, and never pondered over or reminisced about, the sudden shock as it comes back all at once – from a smell, a gust of wind, the way the light catches in the periphery, a word spoken in a certain tone – distorts the original memory. It burns unfiltered, blinding in its severity, a dramatic over-representation.

Maybe there is no good way to remember things. Memory is like a record that can be played only a few times before it starts to deteriorate. At first, the erosion is negligible, but after a while, that hiss we were able to ignore for a time, intensifies, straining and flattening the original version.

To return to the story: Pope – the animal now chasing Bill through the forest – did not remember that he had already met this man when he was a pup. Though we can't know exactly how memory works for wolves, would it surprise us as humans to know that he didn't remember meeting and befriending a man, when man is and always has been the most lethal creature in existence? Assimilate with the assassin, and you become party to your own downfall.

Bill didn't piece together that he'd already met Pope, long ago, when he was a pup, one belonging to a wolf he had come to know well.

TO BE BOTH PET AND PACK MEMBER

After escaping the Fire at Yellowstone, Bill had driven north along the Rockies toward the Canadian border and knew he wouldn't be able to get across without transit permission or employment papers. Overcrowding and overheating in the United States had become severe, and those who couldn't afford to live in temperature-regulated compounds had fled to Canada, where there were more laws prohibiting excessive residential expansions. Canada responded to the "climate refugees" with stricter immigration laws and heavily guarded borders. Still, the borderlands were cooler, and there was no telling how far the Fire would ultimately spread, though it did eventually die out before reaching Great Falls, Wyoming. It had taken two weeks to spread through all of Yellowstone, the largest and hottest fire the region had ever seen. After a month, news outlets began reporting it with a capital *F*.

Many animals fled of their own accord. Bill and the other rangers had done their best to drive out the ones that remained, but many were too weak from months, for some even years of starvation. The position of Yellowstone National Territory Ranger attracted mainly Neo-Abolitionists, as it offered first-hand experience reintroducing animals back to the wild, to live out their lives naturally.

But the extreme climate changes had already taken hold, and Yellowstone was not the wild sanctuary it once was. Migrating birds lingered only several weeks in the summer. They stayed away longer each year and eventually remained in their chosen northern sanctuaries. Beavers overpopulated the lands and changed the ecology of the natural water sources — though many, like the renowned Old Faithful, were already starting to go dry. Deer grazed on whatever grass and shrubbery hadn't been burned up from the intense summer heat, their populations thinning from starvation, leaving little prey except for elk and bison.

The wolves were more creative, though their numbers did ultimately dwindle. Some fled the boundaries of Yellowstone and were either killed by renegade farmers or captured by dog breeders. Disease spread through those who remained. Those packs with the strength and the numbers to hunt were malnourished by already starving prey. By the time the Fire took over the northern boundary, the wolves had disappeared, simultaneously filling Bill with relief and dread. If all the wolves were dead or gone, Bill hoped Shirley was among those who had made it out, and he drove north, wondering if he'd find her.

Or if she'd find him like she always managed before.

The rangers weren't supposed to name the wolves. It made no sense to do such a thing. The wolves had designations so they could be tracked and their behaviors researched, but that was just for the scientists and rangers. Besides, to name something is to take a kind of ownership of it, to assume that there is an emotional kinship or bond. It was the view of the Neo-Abolitionists that it was precisely this human habit of over-association with wolves, and then dogs, which led to their complete disconnection from wild instincts, and the weakening of the entire species.

Generally, Bill agreed, but that was before he met Shirley.

Personal experience always overpowers general moralizations.

~

Less than a year before the Fire, he was on a survey walk along the Geyser Basin, leading out to the Prismatic Spring. Like so much of the natural water in Yellowstone, the spring had started to dry out ten years prior, and now it was a stinging, hot orange wound in the earth, a gummy stew of minerals, far too many parts per million to dissolve in the remaining water. It was an echo of what it once was, a hollow reflection, which Bill knew only from pictures. Waterfalls had become naked cliffs, and rivers were now narrow canyons, and in the places where the rapids once were, water now trickled through the exposed, craggy floor.

But out of hope or habit, Bill continued his ritual survey walks, even though his reports were mostly the same. It was an early morning January day and temperatures were good then, the air coolish with an occasional icy breeze, the presence of the winter season still grasping for position. The grounds had patches of snow that had fallen in the night, now melting around the edges, warmed by the morning sun.

Bill knew a wolf was following him. Usually, the wolves of Yellowstone stayed clear of the rangers, but there was one known as Druid Alpha 2945, the female alpha – the sole remaining alpha – of the longest reigning and now dwindling Druid Pack, that had an unusually curious nature. She would often appear up ahead of wherever Bill was hiking, making herself visible only for a few moments before vanishing back into the woods or over the crest of a hill. A white-chested black wolf, her presence was benevolent, and she never came very close.

Until this January morning, when she did.

The sky was blue, streaked with clouds, and Bill stuffed his hands in his pockets, chilled from the occasional gusts of dewy air. His Stetson blocked the sun from above, but Bill still squinted at the copper-colored grounds. The call of a single crow rang out as it sailed across the sky. Looking up and following its path, Bill's eyes landed near the tree line, far across the Basin, just at the place where a blinding orange desert met the deep, lush green pines.

From far away, the clear appearance of her almost ghostly white-yellow eyes commanded him to stop. Her eyes were terrifying and sentimental at the same time. He had seen that look in a dog long ago, although in the years since, the memory had bound itself with another: That of Shirley. Somehow, the wolf's eyes were, in his mind, Shirley's. It was a melancholic retrieval of a memory too painful to recall accurately, but too wonderful to be entirely forgotten. They stood there looking at each other, and right at the moment when something would distract Bill, like a strong gust of wind, a crow's caw, or an eagle's screech, causing their gazes to break, allowing the wolf a chance for a mysterious escape – nothing happened. Time stretched out, and the two stood there looking at each other from across the sticky geyser.

She started trotting toward Bill, hesitantly but deliberately. Then she turned and galloped back a few paces to the woods, stopping and turning her head to look back. She did this back-and-forth dance multiple times, each time moving slightly farther to the edge of the trees, and Bill realized that she wanted him to follow her.

She'd chosen him.

The wolf stayed a good distance ahead of Bill as he followed her into the forest, but she always looked back to make sure he was still there. She finally came to a stop at the entrance to a large opening in the ground, partially hidden in the brush.

Just at the base of a large fallen tree, roots upturned, was her den, and Bill didn't dare take one step closer.

The wolf huffed and stomped her paws against the ground. She took a step toward the den, looked inside, stepped back, and looked at Bill.

It was an invitation.

In a state of slow-motion, dream-like reality, Bill took one step toward the den, followed by another, until he was crouched down looking at two black wolf pups. They were so small, thin, and whimpering. Bill stepped back and looked at the wolf. He realized that her belly concaved a little too far up into her ribcage for a well-fed wolf. She was hungry, and so were her pups, and in a phenomenal deviation from the norm, she had asked Bill for help. It was his turn to be chosen by a being with eyes and attention that made him feel as special as Shirley had.

For months after, he came back to that spot every week with some carrion that he found on his walks. Starting occasionally and then each time, Bill called her Shirley, and she and her cubs, a little bigger by then, would follow him on his survey walks. They were never alongside him but behind, to the side, in front, always around. When the pups played, Shirley permitted him to play with them, rolling in shady grass, the pups nipping and laughing. Shirley stood by, her distance signaling approval, ready to show teeth the moment they got too rough.

Soon after, the Fire began.

And so, several days out of Yellowstone, the smoke billowing out of a black sky in the rear-view mirror, Bill drove north and watched the trees on either side of the road, increasingly afraid he would never see that galloping black wolf and her two pups again. He drove for hours, craning his neck from side to side until it ached, and when he pulled over to rest, Shirley appeared with her pups, walking down the center of the road. As usual, she was ahead of him.

These three black wolves, as best as Bill could know, were the last surviving members of the legendary Druid Peak Pack, who had existed at Yellowstone for almost 100 years. Shirley looked thin and exhausted from outrunning the fire and smoke, minding the inexperienced pups as she did it. She walked up to him without hesitation this time and lunged, swinging her front paws up on Bill's shoulders. He staggered and dug his heels into the ground to remain upright.

"Easy, Shirley. How you doing there, girl?"

Her ghostly eyes met his, and she licked his face. Her fur smelled of smoke, and her tongue was sandy and dry. She dropped down, lumbering for a few steps until finally sitting on the hot asphalt. With a free hand, Bill broke another protocol: He opened the back of his truck. Shirley broke one too: She stumbled to her feet and allowed Bill to pick her up and place her in the covered hatch. Bill placed the two male pups in with her, and together they continued north, still hoping for refuge and temperance.

They found it in an abandoned cabin for a brief few months, where Bill, Shirley, and her pups were both pet and pack members to one another.

Bill

Bill felt as though his breath had been knocked out of his chest as he stumbled to the ground. The cries of the bull elk had vanished into the forest, and all was quiet except for a low rumble creeping out between the wolf's fangs as he gripped Bill's ankle.

The moment heaved like a wave of blood coursing through an artery. Time swelled and Bill felt it in his ears, almost like a pressure change in the air. His eyes were locked with the wolf's, whose jaw was still fixed, expertly compressing to immobilize, but not to injure. Then something flashed in the wolf's eyes. The slightest twitch, a need to move in a moment of confining heaviness.

The wolf, enraged. Bill, petrified.

They sat there, frozen, and started to remember each other. When a person's life flashes before their eyes, it's not chronological, and it's heavily edited. Bill didn't remember everything that had ever happened to him, and he didn't need to. But as the wolf blinked and removed his teeth from Bill's leg, he remembered when this same wolf had nibbled his ankles as a pup. In those gleaming yellow eyes, the color of a midday sun, he saw the wolf pup whose mother had been Shirley.

Pope

Haah – ehh – zuhh – eee

As Pope held the leg of the tiny creature in his mouth, it made a sound. At first, unrecognizable. It was a wheezing, begging, weak sound. A sound of fear, death, extinction, the sound of a useless thing pleading for its life. As a wolf, Pope did not respond to pleas.

Eee – haah – zuhh

Heeh – zee

He kept his fangs in place but did not bite down, because something about the sound had changed. It had begun to assume a familiar shape. It called his mind back to the kennel and his paw pads felt cold from the memory of the cement. He twitched, recalling the burden of confinement.

Eee – zee

It changed again, and Pope's only response was to soften his eyes. The sound swept him far back before the kennel, to a time before the Fire. It removed him from this place and brought him back to being small, and to being with his mother at Yellowstone, and then later, in a small cabin where he watched shadows dance on a wall in the early mornings. His whole world had changed dramatically, but being a pup, it had been easier to accept. Change isn't scary until one is attached to the expectation of a certain way of life.

Easy.

Easy.

Pope watched the creature transform before his eyes back into a man, his curly hair returning to its bushier state, his arms and legs stalky, his oversized hands, somehow hairier now, pawing the earth, powerful and wild in their movements. He took up a great deal of space now, and his smell mixed with the environment. It was a furless, hairy musky odor, which Pope thought he knew only from a dream.

He was the wild man, and Pope remembered him now.

THE BALLAD OF BILL AND SHIRLEY

Bill

The unusually early spring of Shirley's thirteenth birthday had resulted in a "super bloom" that swept across the entire continent. It was most concentrated in the central states and drifted up into the northeastern United States. The land between housing settlements and industrial compounds turned almost neon, humming with vibrancy. The flowers and foliage were unlike anything that had ever occurred, Madagascar-like in their shocking appearance. They grew over and above themselves, outside their predetermined natural bounds. Roots propagated, the wet internal meat and sap of the tree bursting through the protective outer bark. They pushed up earth and overtook any available space, displacing concrete until workers were forced to dig the trees up, leaving permanent pits. Flowers overpopulated the stems they hung on, and even those grew dense and hairy. Stuffed together and bursting the sepals, technicolor petals hung crowded and large, exposing bulbous ovaries and pollen-coated pistils. A toxic yellow haze hovered everywhere, glimmering in the sunlight like the gases of a hopeful young solar system.

It seemed for a time like the earth was trying to reclaim itself, an overly compensatory burst, as a dying person might experience a moment of intense mental clarity in the midst of their decline. That is, until it started happening every year. Just as winter became known as a time for viral pandemics, the biggest cause of death in summer, next to heat stroke, became allergy-related.

Bill got sick, and his symptoms appeared several days after his experience with Shirley in the Mohonk Reserve. First, it was just the sniffles combined with red and swollen eyes. Then his throat grew raspy, he started wheezing, and his fever spiked. His mother got sick too, and so did his grandmother, and during a news broadcast one evening, the anchor reported that, due to excessive amounts of pollen in the air, cases of anaphylaxis were spreading across the country, and warned people not to go outside, not even during "unlocked" times.

The severity of his symptoms passed after about a week, and although he enjoyed his time reading books, a certain restlessness had replaced his once generous and idle satisfaction of being indoors. His birthday came and went, and when his grandmother recovered from her allergy attack, she baked him a cake that tasted as sweet as it ever did but failed to satisfy a now constant craving for something more satisfying, something he'd only felt in Shirley's presence. He smiled politely as he ate it, the heaviness of the cake momentarily dampening a near-constant restless flutter in his chest.

The pollen counts polluted the air quality every year from then on, starting as early as February. Outside hours were already limited for many, and entirely restricted for some. But Bill never got sick again. Something happened to him that first year. His own allergic reaction seemed to cause his system to fortify. It was as though he went through not only a mental transformation in the Mohonks but also a physiological one. The earth had taken him in and assimilated him.

As the years passed, his parents tried to stop him from going outside. Cases of anaphylaxis were rising, pharmaceutical companies struggled to keep up with the increasing need for medication, and no one could be sure of being safe. Eventually, when it became clear that everyone in his family got sick *except* for Bill, they stopped keeping him inside during the unlocked hours.

The small apartment that Bill and his family lived in had no room for the number of books Bill wanted to read. He'd consumed nearly everything he could as a child, at home, as well as at the library, and still he felt unsatisfied. It wasn't enough for him anymore to read books of fantastical adventures in futures that would never exist, of historical worlds from long ago, of murders and mysteries that required human proximity to even occur, with poetry that he didn't understand, in natural environments that no longer held any earthly possibility.

Shirley's house, on the other hand, was much bigger, and her family had room for lots of books. During his teenage years, he went over to Shirley's house as often as possible, not just to enjoy her collection of books, but to see what she enjoyed in them.

Shirley

"Look, it's like what your grandma talked about once, a *picnic*," Shirley pointed to a page in an art history book, a painting of a naked woman looking directly at the viewer, seated next to men in dark suits. Another woman bathed in the background, framed by trees, and fruits and bread were spilled on the lush ground in the foreground. Shirley's finger lingered over the page, feeling curious to touch the image of the naked woman and not knowing why. She sat on the floor, on the rug in her bedroom, a comforting habit leftover from her days as a much smaller person.

"But she's naked," Bill blushed.

Shirley hunched over the book and started coughing. It was a deep and dry cough, coming straight from the bottom of her lungs, her diaphragm battering her insides in a violent attempt to kick out the offending particles. She was aggravatingly sick, as she was every year around her birthday. The symptoms taxed her body, weakening her already thin frame, and though she would soon turn eighteen, she hadn't grown much since her mid-teens. Her breasts were small, and she had the flushed yet wiry appearance of a girl only just reaching puberty.

Though time might have been neglectful of the rest of her body, it had changed her face. Her cheekbones and jaw were more pronounced, giving her a serious, intense look. Her dark brown hair, once straight and uncomplicated to suit her childhood self, now had a slight wave to it, a flirtatious flip framing her pale face. Her eyes, always green, now had a bit of grey in them, and they shone deeper, like shimmering sedimentary rock pools. When she looked out at the world and at Bill, she felt not just fear*less* anymore, but fear*some*. She craved freedom from her sickly body, to be able to inhabit a vessel that would take her to places she wanted to go, to have experiences she longed for. She wanted that so much, to feel good – she coveted it – and sometimes she felt afraid of what she might do to embody it.

Shirley's coughing wave passed. She wiped her nose with the back of her sleeve and continued flipping through the pages of the art history book. It was a fabric-bound antique copy from the previous century, kept intact from being in climate-controlled interiors. Dust particles danced in the air each time she turned a page. Parts of the fabric had begun to disintegrate and left a gritty coating on her fingers whenever she handled it. Had her parents been awake, they would have made her put it back on the shelf, knowing fully that she'd take it down again after they'd gone to bed.

"People were naked more in the olden days," Shirley said, "the air wasn't so, you know, *itchy*."

Shirley imagined two of the largest green areas of Queens, Flushing Compound Green and Queensborough Bridge Green, and in her mind, they were suddenly scattered with naked people. Pale bodies lay out in the sun, scattered across the lawns, surrounded by hot buildings. She wondered if a soft breeze would feel good against sensitive body parts, and from this thought came a warm, electric wave that began in the soles of her feet, lingered for a moment in her pelvis and lower abdomen, and shot up to the crown of her head, leaving her dizzy and slightly nauseated.

"But there were laws, weren't there?"

Shirley continued turning pages until she reached the one that always made her inhale a little deeper. She looked up at Bill with her stone-green eyes, wider than they were a moment ago. "The law doesn't always let people do what they need to do."

Bill scooted over closer to see the page in the book, and Shirley felt his warmth.

"Was it the law that tied that man to a tree?" Bill asked. "Are those...arrows?"

"No, it was *god*."

"What's *god*?"

Shirley inhaled the smell of Bill, a young and tender scent of sweat and new skin, vibrating in that in-between place that stretches and reforms from the shape of a boy into something like that of a man. She knew the smell of him well, even the smell of his sweat and fire, but it hit her nostrils differently now. His smell had changed and become deeper and more pungent, and though she was sick, it made her feel vibrantly energetic.

"*God* is something that chooses you. You could be out walking one day, in a forest, and then you pass by this tree and suddenly you just have to touch it." Shirley began lightly stroking the green rug she sat on. "So, you touch the tree for a while, feeling how rough it is. But then it doesn't feel rough, it actually feels soft. And you hug the tree and press your body against it and wait for it to grow through certain parts of you."

The painting they looked at was a depiction of the martyr Saint Sebastian. In the painting, he was tied to a tree, dressed in nothing but a loincloth. Though he wore a crown of thorns and had multiple arrows shot through him, he gazed skyward with a look of intense ecstasy. It was one of the paintings that Shirley was most drawn to, although she was uncertain why.

Bill's odor surged through her, and she felt his fingers brush hers.

"But it can't grow through you, because you're not a tree," Bill said, joining her fingers as they danced on the carpet.

Shirley's hand felt incredibly sensitive to his touch, and the fact that her body was hot with allergy symptoms only heightened this. She felt like a red, sensitive rash which produced that unclear feeling of aggravating delight when stroked.

Bill didn't understand the painting, but Shirley insisted and struggled to find the right words. "It's not about *already* being something, it's what happens after you're chosen. You become something else, something more than you were. And you stay that way forever.

"I read in a book that people used to think *god* was inside a certain building, called a *cathedral,* and a certain book called a *bible.* Or that only certain choices, called a *commandment,* were *god,* and other choices were just wrong. People also used to think that *god* was a person. But I don't think so. I think it's something else. Outside, in the air, in a cool breeze on a hot day. Or inside, when you look at someone and suddenly feel like you really know them. Even if you are around them all the time, they change in front of you and become something else. It's not a decision to choose, it's something that comes from another place. And I think that place is *god.*

Shirley turned her thin body toward Bill. "Anyone can choose, or anything, because *god* isn't in one place, it's everywhere," Shirley linked her fingers through his. "Like, here."

Shirley could already smell Bill's slightly sweet breath, and she wanted his face near hers. She wasn't sure what she'd do with it exactly, having seen kissing only in movies. It wasn't something people from two different families did anymore. But allergies weren't contagious, and she wondered if, despite her watery eyes, Bill could see the message she was sending him through them to come closer.

Both keeping their eyes open, Bill placed his lips against hers and froze for a moment. The sensitive wetness of their mouths released a surge in Shirley's body, and she moved in closer, pressing her face against his. Her chest filled like a balloon, and the sensation carried upward into her head, making her feel dizzy, yet determined. Her body felt like it acted of its own accord, continuing on, bringing them both flat on the floor, her warm body on top of his, their lips still connected in strange and thrilling intimacy.

Spring was a time when Shirley felt weak. Every year, the pollen attacked her small body, treating her as a stranger on her own planet. Her taste buds dulled, her ears were plugged, and coughing, sneezing, and high fever spikes interrupted most activities, relinquishing her to a frustrating indoor existence, her only adventures cerebral in nature.

But as Bill kissed her, a part of her she hadn't felt before began glowing to life. It was like a pilot light had been switched on, and then one burner, then all the burners, and then her whole body turned hot and melted. She stopped thinking, compelled by a rising sense of warmth within her. She didn't know what the sensation meant, but she knew it felt good and powerful, so she followed it.

Her body moved on its own, running, devouring, greedily choosing this direction with ordained purpose.

She continued even as Bill mumbled, "Wait, wait a minute, stop, Shirl, what are you doing?"

Once his shock passed, he pushed Shirley off and sat up. Her face was flushed with feverishness and embarrassment. "I thought...you took my hand, though. I thought you were *choosing* me." The energy she'd felt began to waver, replaced again by the crippling fatigue she knew from daily life. She looked at the floor, the reality of what had just happened washing over her, the fog in her mind clearing, mortification replacing the thunderous excitement she'd just felt. Her forehead wrinkled, her chin started shaking, and she began to cry.

Bill reached for her. "No, wait." His face flushed, understanding that he'd just rejected the most tender offering he'd ever received from Shirley. "I'm sorry, I just...I don't know, Shirl. I was surprised. Come back."

But Shirley was already crying, her shoulders quaking, and then the crying became coughing. The spasms intensified, and the muscles and tendons in her neck strained against her already thin frame. Her shoulders were hunched from the force of her abdominal walls contracting, and spit dripped from her mouth, the aggressive coughing making it impossible, not only to swallow but to inhale. It was a loud honking sound she emitted as her body expelled every cubic millimeter of precious oxygen, and it woke her father, who came running into the room.

"Oh my god," her father shouted, "call the doctor! She can't breathe. Shirley? Honey, it's going to be ok." He knelt next to Shirley, who was curled up on the floor, her glossy eyes watching Bill watch her as her body shifted away from a tender moment of fluid passion to a permanent, suffocating spasm.

Her father's eyes darted to Bill. "What the hell did you do, boy?"

Bill, horrified and on the verge of tears, his palms still aching to cradle Shirley's hands, his body longing to feel hers pressed against him once more, bolted up and ran.

He ran until he was home and did not sleep.

Bill

Bill didn't see Shirley anymore, not even at the window. He walked by her house often. Shirley's eighteenth birthday came and went, and eleven months later, so did his, right before his graduation. If she had been there to graduate too, she would have been only just nineteen, the age Bill was the following year when he left Queens.

During Bill's senior year of high school, he happened upon her father walking down the street. Bill started to wave to but stopped himself. He wondered if he held any blame or resentment for what happened – and what exactly happened, he didn't know. Her father looked worn and tired, thinner than Bill remembered. There was a worried, fearful look on his face, nothing like the powerful force of the man who sprinted after Bill and Shirley as they ran with the wolfdog into the woods.

The metal roof of Shirley's old house baked in the summer sun and held up against wind, rain, snow, and hail in the winter storms. The stone front steps grew acid-white during times of drought. These things would have happened anyway, but to have them happen without Shirley's head popping up on the other side of a window, for the steps never to feel the warmth of her feet trod on them, the house looked abandoned.

One day, shortly before Bill left Queens, he noticed a sign on the front door, and for the first time since he was sixteen years old, he climbed Shirley's steps. He read the orange plastic laminated sign fixed to the front door:

THIS PROPERTY IS CONDEMNED
By order of the City of New York and Queens County,
in accordance with Chapter 275B of the Habitation
Development Code, this structure has been condemned
due to extreme unsanitary conditions, structural
deterioration, or abandonment.
It is uninhabitable and entry is hazardous.
NO TRESPASSING

For Bill, even long after he left Queens and went searching for a place where he could feel her nearness, Shirley remained in that house, sixteen years old and a fearless force of nature, weathering the years against a battering world.

HOW TO BE WOLVES TOGETHER

Pope

Summer had just begun to claim its domain when Pope, Hume, and the wild man first set off into the woods, and the heat elevated steadily to unbearable levels.

Sleeping on bristly, yellowed underbrush and sandy, parched earth, it was only in the morning hours, just before the sun peeked over the mountains, that the scorching temperatures receded enough to be tolerable. For weeks, they had only been able to travel at the beginning and end of the days, when the shadows were longest, becoming crepuscular creatures, and sometimes even later into the depths of the night. Though they had traveled north, they couldn't outrun the onset of the heat. During the night, Pope woke often, but in the brief coolness of the predawn hours, all three slept soundly.

Until one night, the heat rose, remained constant, and did not abate, the full moon hanging as a white-hot ember in the suffocating stillness, handing its charge mercilessly back to the sun as day broke.

They had started off much later, exhausted from a night of fitful sleep in the oppressive air. After many hours of traveling, Pope led Hume and the wild man into a deep thicket for the night. Damp and sheltered from the sun, it had preserved a pocket of cool air. The ground had stung the bottoms of Pope's paws, which, at the end of every day, were swollen and raw from trekking on the hot ground, even while keeping to the shadows. Damp and sheltered from the sun, the ground in the thicket was a salve for his tender pads. He nestled himself on the soft dirt and chewed on leaves and grass, both for their water and to settle his stomach, irritated by hunger and thirst.

Hume was next to enter the thicket, and though his body was smaller and nimbler, he seemed every day to recover less quickly from the heat. He sniffed the area and, upon finding a suitable place to rest, he collapsed, his irritated paws tucked awkwardly underneath him. His red, dry tongue hung out of his mouth, and his eyes looked glassy.

In the past few weeks of traveling, Hume had become like a brother to Pope. When tracking prey, Pope had taught Hume how to shadow him. Hume knew that when Pope dropped down in the grass and flattened his ears against his head, he was to mimic him and focus his attention on where Pope's settled. He knew how to detect the slightest muscular and skeletal movements of Pope's body, to know when his attention shifted, or when he was about to switch tactics, to rise, to move. Hume had learned, first, how to follow Pope when he tracked prey, and then how to move independently, acting in a distracting or herding capacity, to help maintain the course of the prey animal. He'd learned how to combine efforts with Pope to tease, torment, and exhaust the animals they tracked, to deliver wounding bites in strategic places, to help Pope ultimately, with his massive jaw, deliver the final, fatal blows.

In the brief and few periods when their stomachs were full, they'd learned to play together. They growled to tease each other and indicate friendliness, they slapped the ground in giddy play, and rolled around, taking each other playfully in their muzzles. Pope, much larger than Hume, had accidentally bitten him too hard on a few occasions and broken the wolfdog's thick skin. He'd licked those wounds and, the next time they devoured a kill, allowed Hume a little more than his usual share. Pope adjusted the strength of his bite, the force behind his frolicking, and accepted Hume as a large pup, one that would never grow to full size.

Pope and Hume had learned how to be wolves together.

When Pope saw the wolfdog's delicate body, frail from dehydration, collapse on the cool earth, he went over to lick his tender, burnt paws. Pope's tongue was just barely dampened from the grass and brush he'd eaten. Hume's panting began to slow, and he dropped his head down and closed his eyes, finally having the energy to curl his body in a more deliberate way. He let out a whining sigh, and Pope wheezed a low, breathy growl in response. The sun's setting rays cut through the thick overstory, illuminating the leaves in silhouette. Pope watched the light glitter off what few droplets of moisture remained in the soil, and the sight of it gave him a waking sense-dream of the smell of fresh dew.

A gentle fluttering of air disturbed the fur in Pope's ears as a crow landed in the thicket, hugged its wings against its body, and tramped gently among the brush. Greyish brown fur, blood, muscle fibers, and fat stuck to its beak and body, leftover from scavenging, and cooked there by the heat of the day. It poked at the ground, looking for water, nibbling at the damp bits of earth it could find. It picked and nibbled and padded over to Pope and Hume, where it fearlessly began nibbling at their fur, finding small bugs, bits of dried sweat, and dead skin. The two remained in their position and allowed the crow to go about its business. Neither species had any interest in disrupting the other.

The crow emitted a high-pitched croak, a small particle of communication, testing the climate and interest of Pope and Hume.

Hrr – Krr – Hrr – aaww

Its breath smelled sweet and metallic, surely of squirrel, and Pope lifted his head and huffed, ruffling the crow's feathers.

Hh – uuhh

Gh – uuhh

The crow tilted its head on an axis and croaked, with each puff of air filling the space with the dense, iron smell of blood and flesh. Hume lifted his head and huffed with a parched, hungry throat.

Hmm – uuhh

The crow opened its mouth and vomited partially digested squirrel meat onto the ground. It was a gesture symbolic of a once strong hunting partnership between wolves and crows, now rendered nearly obsolete by scarcity and an obliterating thermal weather front that seemed to eat up all other seasons. For the starving and exhausted wolves, the crow served the role of both hunter and scavenger, offering what little food it had found, even at the risk of its own survival. It was a sign of a failing ecosystem, one in which animals were forced to obliterate and reform existing boundaries, to nurture each other so that some of them may survive.

It was not enough food for Pope and Hume, but they licked the bloody puddle anyway, and then dozed.

The sound of snapping branches and rustling leaves awoke both Pope and Hume from their fitful naps. The wild man lumbered in from the sun-streaked forest, swirls of hot air from his body dissipating as he entered the coolness of the protected thicket. He smelled oily with the stink of dehydrated sweat.

In the time they'd been together, Pope had watched the wild man grow taller and thinner, and his hair become bushier and overgrown, like the tops of trees sprouting furiously in the new summer air. He walked softer now, and to Pope, it looked as though his feet didn't meet the ground, but rather plunged into it with each step. Like a tree afoot, he'd sprouted roots and embedded himself. But as a man, he could still walk, and Pope could sometimes see tendrils of earthy ligaments dangling from his legs as he moved through the woods.

His face had darkened, and his features were almost imperceptible, save for his eyes, which had become bulbous, his once green irises now vanished into the sooty milk-colored whites. His musk was stronger with layers of sweat, overgrown nails, and skin. Occasionally, he made the sounds Pope knew, *eee – zee, eee – zee,* but Pope had taught him how to huff and growl, and, when not completely silent, using his energy only to breathe, the wild man made the sounds of a new kind of human.

Bill

After the elk stalking incident, Bill had shouldered his rifle and used it only as a primitive tool now, something for hammering, punting, a walking instrument to steady himself, a pole for reaching food in high places, whatever hadn't been baked and spoiled by the sun. As the weeks passed, Bill kept his distance behind the wolf and Boy, sometimes taking as long as several hours to reach a place suitable enough for the night's shelter.

He did not take initiative in any stalk again, and only acted when the wolf gave him deliberate instructions, conveyed with grunts, short, quick howls, dances, and bites to Bill's ankles. When called upon, he killed without distraction and used brute force. Bill had learned how to let the wolf claim his role as the natural leader, and in this way, he felt he'd achieved something no other environmental activist had: It was the wolf who had rehomed him, and not the other way around.

After leaving the kennel and traveling north into the Yukon, Bill had seen makeshift shelters built by climate refugees. They were constructed out of smaller boulders arranged to function as a single, bearing wall, supporting a web of branches and dried leaves, acting as a canopy. They looked like the witches' dens he used to read about in Shirley's books. She wanted to be one of these, a *wild woman,* she called them, drying meat in the sun and running in the woods half-naked with a wolf by her side.

Some shelters had been there since before the laws turned strict, but others were newer, built by those who couldn't afford the technology to outfit their homes for the increasingly drastic changes in the ecosystem and climate.

They were all abandoned, as the shelters, which served as a gentle respite in the summers, quickly became inadequate when the northern winter had descended. Bill didn't know where the people had gone, but the skeletons of the homes they'd created left a sobering reminder that the remains of the former inhabitants might be buried somewhere nearby.

Another chilling thought crossed Bill's mind: If they'd frozen solid in the winter, their corpses would still have flesh on them, flesh that could be dried in the sun and eaten when prey was scarce. Bill's mouth began to water with the prospect.

Although Bill had spent many days at a time out in the wilds of Yellowstone, these past months were the first time he'd felt truly immersed in the environment since he was a boy. When he and Shirley had run away into the woods, neither had known anything about survival. It was lucky a rescue helicopter had found them, although they both got sick anyway. And Shirley, far sicker.

For Bill, she didn't die. She just disappeared, and that's not quite the same thing.

He knew a lot more since their attempted childhood runaway. He knew how to start a fire and how to dig a well for water. He knew on sight which branches and tree limbs were hollow, eaten from the inside by termites or fungus, and which were solid enough to make shelters, and which were solid but dry, and which were sap-logged, good for burning. He knew which plants produced the most pollen, how to harvest it, dry it, and eat it to fortify himself during the months when the risk of anaphylaxis was higher.

He had also eaten more meat in this time than he ever had in his life, and though it never once occurred to him that he might eat human meat, he didn't have the energy to feel surprised at how easily it came to his mind. Hunger has a way of dulling morality, making it seem distant, abstract, and highly modular. It functions as a reeking reminder that an empty stomach spasming inside a withering body is indifferent to any intellectual cause.

Shirley's idealism was a vague memory to him now, echoes of a version of himself that he could never return to. Just as he knew more about how to survive in the wild with no help from the human world, he saw how frightful he'd had to become in order to live that way. To kill with his bare hands, to eat a living creature, to look into its eyes as its soul drained away, the vital force with which it fought against death with every cell of its being. He ate that and liked how it felt to feed every cell of *his* being.

In his transformation, he'd discovered a true wildness within him, a feral violence essential to the development of every successful life form on earth.

The wolf and Boy lifted their heads only slightly as Bill entered their protected thicket. They looked weak, hungry, and exhausted. The temperature had been steadily rising, and it lingered long after the sun set. It was changing the very ground they walked on, and Bill felt it through the soles of his shoes. Even though they tried to move only in the most dense parts of the forest, with the most coverage, Bill still wondered how the wolf's and Boy's paws were handling the perpetually warming ground.

Bill approached the wolf and groaned as best he could. *Hoo – ff*

The wolf responded. *Pp – hauu – pp*

Bill took out a canteen with some water he'd filtered from a stream that day. It was warm at the time, but hopefully, in the hours of being strapped to Bill's torso, it had at least been brought down to body temperature. He took a swig himself and then poured some gently over the heads of the wolf and Boy, and their tongues lapped furiously as the water dripped into their mouths.

A faint slant of warm air wafted into the thicket and interrupted the chill, followed by a prickling sound outside. A second warm breeze followed the first, and it seemed to expand in the space between the trees and brush. It was dark now, but the air grew hot and very still, encasing Bill's body. It was as though another person had entered the thicket, invisible yet large, vacuuming up all the air and vitality of the place. He felt the baked ground through the soles of his boots, similar to a midday heat, only now it was well past sunset, stars already appearing in the sky. In an instant, all moisture seemed to dry up, and Bill's mouth went pasty. He looked at the wolf who had stood up, and Boy, who was still half-seated. Both had their ears pricked up in attention and were panting, dry tongues hanging out of their mouths. The thicket didn't feel like protection anymore. It was now an oven.

A wildfire had started outside.

THE END

The forest flashed past Pope's periphery as he sprinted.

He was filled with a primal terror, his mind emptied of all thoughts other than the ones that told him to run far and fast. His paws drummed the earth rhythmically, and the night air rushed past him, slowly clearing of smoke. The air became dense with moisture, and he could breathe more easily. Pope's panicked run evolved into something of a madness, a crazed dash of elation. It was the second time in his life that a fire had spurred him, and as he sped through the forest, driven purely by instinct, he was a whole primal beast. In that run, he was the kind of animal he might have been had the Druid Pack not been forced to flee from the Yellowstone Fire, had his brother not died, had winter not died, and had the natural order not been dislodged from its grooves. He panted, his sprint slowing to a trot, and he walked heavily through the darkness.

The smell of smoke was as distant as a memory now, and after a time, the trees cleared, and the land opened to a long, narrow lake, surrounded by spruces. The air temperature dropped sharply, surrounding him clear and cool, like a pouch of the previous season preserved, and the feeling of this shift induced an energetic frenzy in Pope. He took a gasp of the refreshing air into his mouth and turned his gaze skyward, seeing the moon low bathe the scene in a fresh, silvery-blue light, and felt for a moment as if he were just waking from a long, hot sleep.

Pope trotted along one side of the lake until the brush became too thick to pass, and then back down the same side, following the curve which looked as though it might bring him around to the other side, until the brush cut him off again. Circling back to the thick of the forest, he found a place to settle for the rest of the night, his tired legs making the decision for him. The wild man and Hume had not appeared, and Pope had lost them in his frantic flight away from the smoke. He slept immediately and did not see the moon travel across the sky and eventually vanish below the horizon.

He awoke just as a pale blue began to emerge from the indigo of early morning. Focusing his eyes on the edge of the lake, he saw a small herd of deer drinking. Only a few seasons ago, the deer would have bolted at the nearness of him. Instinctively, he tried to identify the weakest of the pack, the one he would plan to isolate and prey upon. But Pope had no other to give instructions to, and the deer knew it. Because he was alone, they were unafraid and didn't flinch as he approached the lake to drink in their vicinity. The water was the coolest thing to touch his tongue in weeks, a mildness unspoiled by the relentless heat. It washed away any remaining taste of smoke in his mouth, the memory of the fire drifting further into the reaches of his mind.

As he drank, his eyes focused, and he saw his own reflection. There was a wolf. He had never thought about how *wolf* looked on him, but now that he'd observed creatures that looked like him, only without the wolf, he saw it. His eyes, startling now in comparison to the soft eyes of Hume, were so yellow, they seemed less like a color and more like the blinding reflection of the sun off placid water. Pope blinked and tried to see if he could make his eyes go soft. He opened his jaw and let his tongue fall out, as he'd seen Hume do sometimes with the wild man. It didn't work. He shook his head and let his tongue flap. He exhaled sharply. He took one paw and wiped his brow. He licked the water and watched himself obscure. When it stilled, the intense yellow eyes of a wolf appeared once again.

He finished drinking and looked for the deer, who had wandered closer to the woods to graze. He watched them eat calmly and slowly, and desperation gripped his insides. He whined softly and unintentionally, a deep wish breaking the surface tension of him: He wished for another wolf, another to hunt with, to coordinate an attack, to eat, to play, and to sleep. He wished for the culture of the wolf, the culture he carried inside himself and would never truly be able to impart. He'd taught Hume everything he could, but Hume was not a wolf. He could imitate, but he could not understand.

They played like puppies, and Pope felt the absence of a feral partner, one who could share ownership and primal dominance in their own territory. Maybe in a more fruitful ecosystem, they could have become a stronger pack, but evidence spoke loudly to the fact that

Pope was alone – Hume had not been able to run as fast.

In the months before Pope had been captured, he'd howled into the treetops, hoping the echo would find other wolves. He'd never gotten a response and never heard any lone howls calling for him. That is, until the humans had taken him, until he'd howled again, and Hume's answer had met his lonely ears with the same sounds but in a strange accent. Pope didn't know if Hume and the wild man had made it out of the fire, and his nose was too strained from the smoke to seek them out. He considered this, albeit a distanced consideration, as the deer were suddenly far more interesting to him.

Like him, they were wild. Although as his prey, in relationship to him, they held an opposite yet equal understanding of what that meant.

Pope nibbled some grass and watched them, and if they were aware of his presence, they didn't show it. He walked closer and looked at their brown fur and brown eyes. The way they stood, separate yet together, signaling one another through their ease of being. It was this basic connection that was barren from Pope's life, one that he'd tried to foster within the strange threesome, but never quite achieved, because it was altogether wrong. No matter how much he'd built with Hume and the wild man, they were not of his world, and he was not of theirs. They had worked hard to create a culture of their own, but it lacked the innate history borne and sustained in every wolf pack, and therefore, it was fallible and frail.

Pope jumped in front of one of the deer, startling it, flopped his tongue out, and bowed. He slapped the ground with his paws, and the deer took several steps back. Pope lunged forward and, instead of biting to wound, nipped playfully at its ankles. It trotted away a short distance. He overtook the deer and ran in circles, yelping and groaning before finally stopping, panting, waiting, and hoping for a reply.

For a few moments, the deer did nothing, remaining frustratingly unresponsive to Pope's unrestrained attempts to communicate. Then all of them suddenly looked up, and just past him. Pope saw their eyes sharpen simultaneously, their ears prick, and they turned and bolted as one into the forest. From behind him came a padding and a rustling of leaves. Pope turned to see the wild and formidable eyes of a wolf, startlingly now in their unfamiliarity to him, as it emerged from the spruce trees. Morning dew shook off the needle-pointed tips of his black fur as he bristled.

Pope had not met with another wolf in many seasons. Though his body eagerly wanted to erupt with a cacophony of signals in hopes of communication, he stilled himself, pawed at the ground, opened his mouth, and grunted. The black wolf remained motionless. From the trees, another wolf emerged. The first jerked his head in the direction of the other, but never took his wide-eyed stare off Pope. The wolf had recently eaten, and the smell of metal excited Pope's nostrils. He paced quickly a few steps left and right, and then bowed for a moment, anticipating contact. Standing up again, he barked, surprised at the anxiously high tenor of his sound.

An answer came, but not from the black wolf.

Hume came bounding out of the forest in response, giddy at the sight of Pope and blissfully unaware of his surroundings, unable to smell the fear building in the air.

Hume barked, but it wasn't until the first crunch of the wild man's step into the clearing by the lake that the black wolf's ears flattened and his upper lip curled, revealing sharp and glistening incisors. His shoulder blades pulled together, and he began to grunt sharply, and the grunt became a low growl. His head shifted subtly yet clearly, looking from Pope, to Hume, to the wild man, his neck pulsating with each meaty-smelling, steaming exhale. He began grunting again and was not loud, not trying to send his call the great distance of a howl, but the intention of the sound was clear: It was an alarm meant only for the nearest members of the pack, the signal of a threat, the call to organize for a territorial standoff.

Pope stood up, closed his mouth, focused his eyes, and felt his insides harden. Theirs was a makeshift pack, unnatural in its very existence, yet forced into being by necessity and the reality of circumstance. Though Pope had taught them what he could about organization, stalking prey, and taking their places within his pack, they had not experienced a cardinal fight for the right to exist and the right to belong together. And there was no right given in nature except to those who viciously seized it. Three more wolves trotted authoritatively out of the forest, and with the lake behind them, Pope, Hume, and the wild man were cordoned off by four sets of flaming yellow eyes.

The black alpha did not crouch and did not inch forward with trepidation, but instead walked upright, directly toward Hume. Hume whined anxiously, and after the first few steps of the black wolf, started with hesitancy toward the trees. Pope turned his head and huffed angrily each time Hume lunged off in the direction of the forest, and Hume obeyed, remaining uneasily in place as the black wolf approached.

Pope walked toward the wolf, who looked similar to him except that, unlike Pope, who had prematurely grizzled around the mouth, he also appeared well-fed and healthy. If he hadn't seen his brother die of distemper, he might have hoped this was him. A part of him did anyway, because a wolf is a half-animal without its family, and whatever else dies first, hope is always last.

The two wolves faced each other with uncertainty, from a distance. They stalked a few paces in one direction, and a few paces in another, eyes fixed, a pink line exposed over their fangs as they growled deeply at one another. Hume and the wild man stood nervously nearby and did not intervene. This was a conversation only Pope could understand, and his own growl held a message for the black wolf alone.

But the message needed to be conveyed in a language Pope hadn't been able to speak since his final, funereal utterances in the moments before the bodies of his mother and brother took up their terminal resting places in nests of blood-colored leaves. It was a way of speaking that Hume and the wild man couldn't quite understand, and because of that, Pope had required himself to dampen it, soften it, lower and raise the tone appropriately, even making puppy-like sounds when needed. It was because of these adjustments that he'd been able to teach them how to function and survive together. And it was because of these adjustments, which had become second nature to him over the months, that what the dew-strewn black alpha heard was something in a strange dialect, delivered in an unfamiliar accent, one that did not exist in the natural world as he knew it.

That made it dangerous.

The wild man called out as Hume succumbed to his anxiety and sprinted off into the woods, and the black wolf righted himself again. Again, he grunted strong, guttural puffs of air: the alarm signal, just as before. The other wolves encroached and forced the wild man and Pope farther apart. The wild man darted away, back toward the forest, unknowingly giving the wolves an easier hunt.

With a lunge, Pope bit the alpha on the leg. Not with anger, or even with warning, but to grab his attention, to indicate that a mistake had been made. He barked again, another high-pitched puppyish bark, forgetting that a grown wolf – an alpha, as he was – would never signal to another alpha in this way. They were rivals, and in his months of isolation, followed by time spent with his foreign family, Pope had forgotten how to hold power in his native tongue. He had developed a kindness necessary to his situation and suddenly found himself in a setting where it held little sway.

The alpha's face rippled as he snarled at Pope, lunging and flashing his teeth in the air, spittle flying with rage at Pope's interference. His eyes were the same blinding yellow as Pope's were, and yet they could not see Pope as what he was: A wolf who had used his heritage to generate another iteration of survival.

Three wolves taunted, lunged, and snarled at the wild man as they drove him back into the woods, stumbling and helpless. Hume had vanished into the forest in a panic, and Pope was held in place by the alpha, his brother in rivalry. As he watched the bristling fur, the abundant and odorous breath hovering in the air, and the black pupils vigilantly fixated on him, he realized he saw more fear in these eyes than he'd ever seen in the humans who'd captured him months ago.

It was why he couldn't contact the wolfish animals the way he'd wanted to, and why the humans had run from him. It was why he played with his reflection in the pond, waiting to see a change. In a state of enhanced desperation, he'd found no form of contact except for wolf-like creatures that didn't form packs, that didn't hunt for their food, that were soft and playful because they didn't need to manage their own survival.

The attempt at contact had initially failed, but he'd found a way with Hume. In the special task of identifying meaningful ways to communicate between the dialects, he'd been forced to confront his own wildness. He saw it clearly now, as no wolf would ever need to, and because he saw it, it was gone from him. He was a peculiar hybrid, an intruder no longer familiar to this space, and there had been no other to watch him change, and to understand. He was more than a wolf now, and this made him not enough of one, and though he longed for it with desperate intensity, the black wolf in front of him would never hear his call.

He watched as the shadows of the forest swallowed the shape of the wild man, growing smaller and translucent until he vanished entirely. Pope tilted his head and looked skyward. As if riding on an unbroken gust of wind, a murder of crows soared upward in effortless cooperation and vanished over the tops of the trees. His howl began low and gravelly, cracking into a higher, aching siren as it echoed throughout the wood.

Acknowledgements

Writing this novella began awkwardly, sitting alone at my desk, teetering on the edge of paralyzing self-doubt, driven by imagination and the sheer force of will to expand a single-character short story into a larger world that I, and hopefully my eventual readers, could believe in. But in the haze and uncertainty of it, there were the people to whom I reached out, who answered my call, and without their support, this book would never have become a reality: My MFA cohort and professors; the Vienna Writers' Club; Ted Flanagan; Brenda Copeland; Ta-wei Chi; every friend, near and far, who volunteered to read my first draft; Bill Lawrence at Broken Tribe, who took a chance and gave Pope and the wild man a home; and my mother, who read every word, twice. I thank you all, most sincerely.

I'd also thank the wolves, if I could. Their fierce loyalty, familial nature, and ability to form new bonds and learn from one another are profoundly fascinating traits. I'm grateful to the research and writings of Jim and Jamie Dutcher, and Brad A. Bulin, among many others, for introducing me to these magnificent creatures.

Finally, to Jack London, and to his Buck, for giving us a timeless love story between man and wild, that shatters and thrills me with each reading.

THE AUTHOR

Eleanor Keisman is an American writer, born in New York. After dropping out of high school, she worked her way up through community colleges in Honolulu, Denver, and upstate New York, finally transferring to Stony Brook University on Long Island, where she studied Fine Arts, but ultimately earned her BA in Liberal Arts from The New School in Manhattan. She left the US and spent over a decade living, studying, and working in France, Czechia, Poland, China, and Austria. Her academic career continued at the University of Vienna, where she studied German and English linguistics. She then worked for a legal tech startup as a bilingual copywriter and marketing consultant (earning an MBA in the process) and an educational NGO, organizing international exchange internships. She holds an MFA in creative writing from Drexel University, where she was the newsletter director and poetry reader for the MFA literary journal, *Paper Dragon.* She co-organizes an English-language writing group in Vienna, Austria, where she lives. Her short stories, poetry, and essays have appeared in *Litro Magazine, The Bangalore Review, Tough Crime, Last Stanza Poetry Journal,* and others. *New Animal* is her first novella.